D1015796

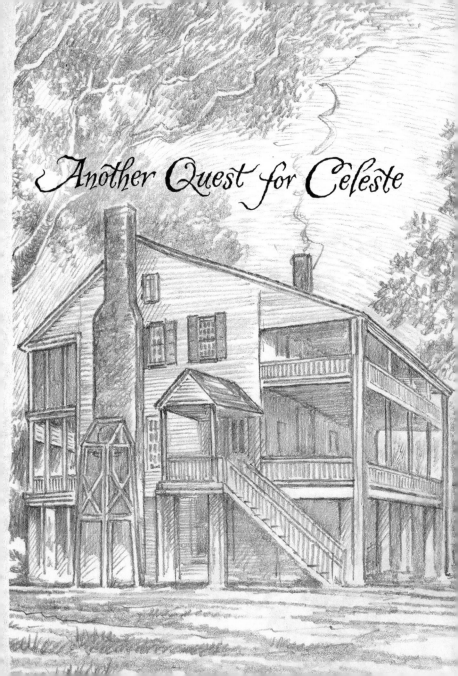

Another Quest for Celeste

HENRY COLE

Another Quest for Celeste

KATHERINE TEGEN BOOKS
An Imprint of HarperCollins Publishers

TETON COUNTY LIBRARY
JACKSON, WYOMING

Katherine Tegen Books is an imprint of HarperCollins Publishers.

Another Quest for Celeste
Copyright © 2018 by Henry Cole

All rights reserved. Printed in the United States of America.

No part of this book may be used or reproduced in any manner whatsoever without written permission except in the case of brief quotations embodied in critical articles and reviews. For information address HarperCollins Children's Books, a division of HarperCollins Publishers, 195 Broadway, New York, NY 10007.

www.harpercollinschildrens.com

ISBN 978-0-06-265812-8

17 18 19 20 21 CG/LSCH 10 9 8 7 6 5 4 3 2 1
❖
First Edition

CONTENTS

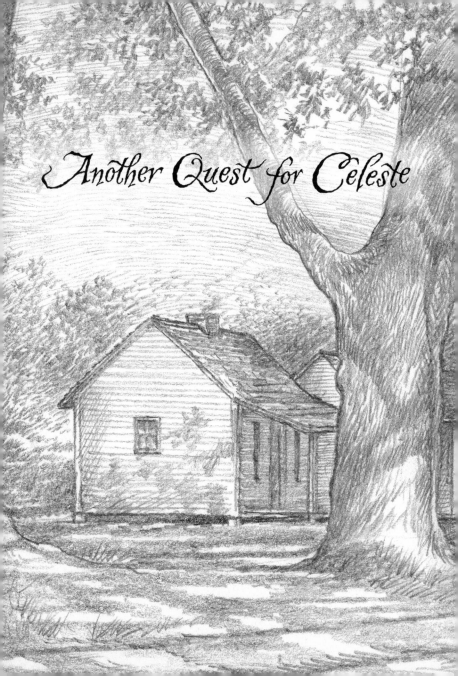

Another Quest for Celeste

CHAPTER ONE

Leaving Oakley

Celeste was jolted awake.

Her cozy spot deep inside the packed cotton bolls pitched and dropped, then pitched again. Though muffled by the mass of cotton, she could hear the groan and creak of wagon bed boards and horse harnesses, swaying and rumbling and clinking.

She poked her pink nose out of the enormous bale of cotton and peeked at the scene below. Two acorn-colored horses were pulling the cotton wagon down the lane, away from Oakley Plantation. Above the treetops, she could see curls of smoke from the brick chimney of the kitchen. It was breakfast time.

At a bend in the sandy road, the barns and chimney top disappeared from view.

Celeste was being carried away from her home.

She felt panicky. She considered jumping, and climbed out onto the side of the mound of cotton, her claws digging into the white fibers. The sand-and-crushed-oyster-shell road was far below.

She clambered on top of the heavy canvas tarp.

"Giddyap!" a voice called. "C'mon, Ginny!" Celeste turned to see two boys sitting at the front of the wagon, one holding a long stick, the other munching a fig.

"Ginny's lazy," the boy with the stick said.

"Aw, she's all right," the second boy replied. "We ain't in no hurry. The packer ain't leavin' before we get there."

Packer? Celeste thought. *What's a packer, and how far is it?*

They drifted past pecan trees and fencerows laced with elderberry bushes. She glanced down; the road was slipping bit by bit beneath the wagon as the horses plodded along. Her beloved dollhouse home in the attic was getting farther and farther away.

Celeste's whiskers twitched with anxiety as she scrambled back and forth across the swaying cotton.

Just then, a shadow flickered across the wagon

and Celeste felt the flutter of wings nearby.

"What," chirped a familiar voice, "are you doing *here*? Are you crazy, riding on top of a cotton wagon?"

Celeste felt an enormous surge of relief as she saw her friend Violet come in for a landing, her soft brown feathers fluffed up in excitement.

"Am I glad to see you!" Celeste squeaked.

"How did you manage to get up here?"

"Last night, I was out looking for food. I shouldn't have strayed so far from the house, but I ended up near the wagon, and I . . ."

"This wagon was sitting all the way over by the barn!" Violet interrupted.

"I know. And it was too far to race back when I saw the house cat skulking about. I made it up into the cotton, then just stayed the night."

Violet clucked encouragingly. "Well, maybe I can find Lafayette, and he can help us out."

"Lafayette! Of course!" Celeste cried out. Her osprey friend was big enough to carry her home. "No telling where he is this morning, but I bet he can help." She relaxed a bit, feeling hopeful.

"I'll go right now. He must be somewhere along the river. It may take me a while, but I'll find him, Celeste. Don't worry."

"When you find him, just follow the road back.

Keep following the road until you find me," Celeste squeaked up. "And thanks, Violet!"

With a quick flick of wings, Violet became a speck in the air as she flew off to find Lafayette.

The wagon rattled down the road, Celeste clutching the canvas.

CHAPTER TWO
Mississippi Wharf

Celeste sat at the top of the cotton bales, looking ahead, her heart racing. The live oaks, gums, and tupelos reached from either side of the road, forming a green tunnel. In places, the shady road was dappled with morning light, dotting across the oyster shells and cream-colored sand.

Her mind was racing, too. The woods and fields around Oakley stretched for hundreds of miles in all directions. The river was vast, with countless creeks and channels; Lafayette could be anywhere, in any direction. He could be sitting in the shadow of some great tree, preening, or soaring over the river, which was nearly a mile wide. Violet would have to scour dozens of square miles; she was just a dot in all of that expanse . . . two tiny eyes searching for a single osprey.

"If anyone can find Lafayette, it's Violet," Celeste said out loud, trying to reassure herself.

After a while, the midmorning sky appeared as the trees thinned out and the road widened. The two boys driving the wagon began talking and gesturing excitedly.

"There it is!" one shouted.

The boy with the stick pulled on the reins. "Whoa . . ." he said, and the wagon slowed and pulled into a crowded throng. Dozens of people were gathered near a large wooden platform that stretched in front of them. The trees had given way to a broad expanse of sky, and Celeste saw a river stretching out in front of her.

Lafayette had taken her on a ride over a river, weeks before. This had to be the same one. The Mississippi!

Celeste gulped. She had never seen so many
people. They were everywhere, shouting
and greeting one another, giving orders, taking orders,
haggling, bargaining,

laughing, and swearing. Some wore fancy clothes—
dark wool suits and top hats glided through bright
red and yellow calico dresses. Some carried
lace-trimmed parasols. Others were
dressed in rags and were

barefoot. Everyone was busy, moving in a cacophony of rhythm and chaos.

And there were enormous piles of goods of every sort and kind: sacks of rice and beans and flour, bales of rope and tobacco, stacks of wooden planks and shingles, bolts of cloth, bushels of oats and corn, and casks of cider, cherry bounce, whiskey, molasses, and lard.

And mountains of cotton bales.

"Whoa!" came another shout from one of the boys, and the wagon came to a halt. With a sudden boom, a large wooden ramp slammed down onto the back of the wagon. Celeste watched in terror as several men began pushing and heaving at the heavy bales of cotton, first one and then another. She was pitched forward, then backward as her bale began rolling off the wagon. She leaped across to another bale just in time.

"Next!" came a shout. Celeste looked about in

a panic, leaping from one cotton bale to another as each was rolled off the wagon and onto the loading dock.

Finally, there was one bale left, with Celeste trying to dig into it to find a hiding place in the cotton fibers.

"Last one!" a man barked out, and Celeste felt herself turn upside down and head over claws as the bale was flipped over and over.

"Ooomph!" she squeaked as the bale was rolled and flipped again and again, finally knocking her off. She landed on the ground, winded and dazed.

The ponderous bale was pushed on, and Celeste found herself on the wide wooden planks of the docking platform. There were dozens and dozens of feet and legs, moving and running this way, that way. She quickly took note of the numerous cats on the dock, some dozing in the shade of the wagons, some

sniffing, some observing the busy scene and wisely staying out of the way. A large dog lounged on the cool side of a shed.

She squeezed easily between the slats of a crate of apples. She took another glance at the sky, straining in vain to discover Lafayette's flapping figure overhead.

Everything had happened so quickly. Celeste's head was spinning. In a short time, she had gone from her quiet and safe attic home to the crazy and chaotic world of trading day on a Mississippi wharf.

Her ears buzzed as people shouted, horses whinnied, and gulls cried out. There were hundreds of new smells: the sweet scent of newly cut pine boards mixed with the sour odor of human bodies in wool clothing, sweating horses, rotting vegetables and fruits, curing hides, and hemp.

And swirling through all the other smells was that of the ever-present and pervasive Mississippi, pungent and rich and earthy. It wound around and crept into every crevice and crack.

Celeste crouched among the apples, gazing through the crate slats at the immense, broad expanse of water. She looked up, and saw Lafayette's silhouette against the sky. She also saw the tiny shape of Violet hovering overhead, searching for her. But just as she started to leap out into the open, a set of boots clomped up to the crate, and she heard a shout.

"Hey! Boy! Get these apples on the boat! Be quick!"

Celeste felt her stomach sink as the crate of apples was lifted aloft and then carried up a ramp onto a boat that was docked nearby. With a scraping thud, the crate slid onto the deck of the boat, and soon after, another one just like it was jammed alongside. More crates were piled on top.

Hours passed as crates and barrels and tons of other supplies were carried onto the flatboat. Celeste's view was obstructed, but she could hear the men shouting and the clomping of boots up and down the boat ramp.

Suddenly, there was a tremendous noise, and everything jerked. She wiggled and maneuvered her way through the crates until at last she could poke her nose between the slats of the crate and out into the sunshine. At one end of the deck, she could see the tops of mammoth wooden paddles rising out of the water and then rolling back down, and hear

the sound of sloshing, splashing, spilling river water. The sight was colossal but magical.

The crate seemed to be moving. She now saw that the tree line of the shore was getting farther away.

She was on a boat, heading up the Mississippi.

CHAPTER THREE
Rosebud

Celeste scanned the sky. There were gulls and crows and turkey vultures soaring overhead, their squawks drowned out by the roar of the paddles and cascading water. But no more sign of Lafayette, nor of Violet.

"Lafayette will never find me in here," she squeaked to herself.

Suddenly, she saw the large, worn paws of a dog wander slowly down the deck and then stop. A wet, black nose started poking and nudging around the apples with loud, snorting sniffs. The nose got closer and closer to her crate. Celeste huddled up against the apples.

Then a dark brown eye appeared only inches away, looking at Celeste among the crimson apples. The nose sniffed again, then the eye returned. Celeste didn't move a whisker.

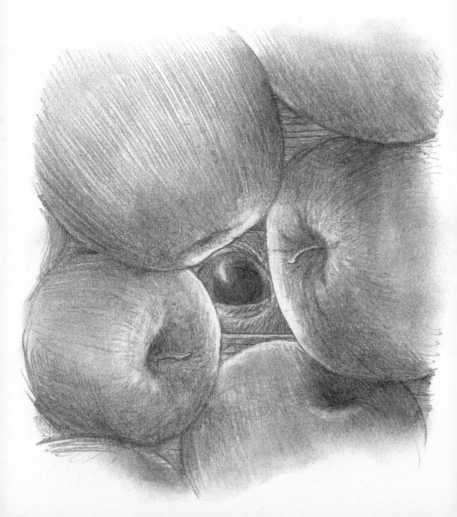

"All right . . . I know you're in there," a rough voice rumbled. "You might as well come out, or else I'll have to get the proper authorities to come 'round."

Celeste gulped. "Are you speaking to me?" she squeaked over the apples.

The brown eye softened. "Oh, you're just a mouse," the dog said. "I thought you might be something dangerous. You don't smell like a regular mouse."

Celeste was relieved but cautious. The dog seemed more like a gentle giant than a rough beast. "Are you going to hurt me?" she asked.

"Nah. You're hardly a mouthful anyway!" the dog answered. "Come out here and let me get a look at you."

Celeste crept over the slippery round apple skins and emerged into the daylight of the boat deck. She looked up at the large dog that towered over her. His honey-colored fur was worn out at the elbows and graying at the muzzle. One ear was shorter than the other, having been nearly ripped off by a fierce raccoon years before.

Her heart softened when she saw that he stood on only three legs; a hind leg was missing.

The old dog looked down at Celeste curiously, but with a little smile.

"You're not the usual kind of mice we get here," he said. "You got white feet! Not the typical run-of-the-mill gray mouse."

Celeste smiled shyly. "My name is Celeste," she replied.

"Name's Rosebud," the old dog replied. "Now, don't laugh. It's the name that was given me."

"I like it," said Celeste.

The dog chuckled and looked at Celeste appreciatively. "Well, thank you muchly, but I would have preferred a more dignified name, if given the choice. Something like Vesuvius. I heard that one once . . .

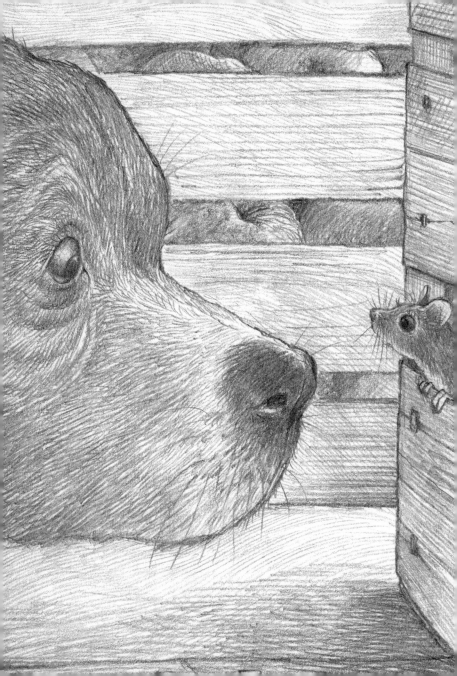

the name of a steamboat. Or Comet."

"Steamboat?"

"Yep, same as this one," Rosebud said. "We're headin' up the river, all the way to Louisville! Should be quite a trip. I've made it twenty-nine times already," the dog added proudly. He looked quizzically at Celeste. "What's wrong, Missy? Your eyes are wider than the Mississippi in springtime."

"I . . . I've got to get off of the steamboat!" Celeste stammered. She looked across the vast expanse of water at the low line of trees that clutched at the distant riverbank. Home was surging away with every heavy swoosh of the giant steam-driven paddles. "I've got to get off somehow!"

Rosebud grinned. "Sit tight," he said. "The *Paducah Queen* will take us to Louisville and back to St. Francisville, all in one piece."

"*Paducah Queen?* What's that?" Celeste asked anxiously.

"The name of this steamboat, naturally. It's takin' us upriver."

Celeste gasped. "Upriver?"

The old dog laughed. "You have more questions than a thunderstorm has raindrops. Well, sure . . . We'll stop in Natchez, and Memphis, and Louisville . . . well, let's see, them's the big stops, but there are all sorts of little stops along the way, too. Bayou Sara, Bayou Feliciana, Ba . . ."

"I'll never get back home!" Celeste exclaimed. She started scrambling nervously over the deck planking, then back into the apples, then over Rosebud's paws.

"Now hold on, there," Rosebud drawled. "You'll be okay. We'll getcha back home. And there ain't nothin' you can do about it now, anyhow. We'll be headin' upriver all night."

"But how will I ever . . . ?"

"Now, you just settle down. Enjoy the ride,"

Rosebud interrupted gently. "There's lots to see." He nodded at the scene spreading before them, and Celeste relaxed a bit with the dog's quiet calm.

The sun was getting lower in the western sky, spreading a gold-and-scarlet icing on angel food clouds. A dark line of trees on the shore silhouetted against the horizon. Even though the churning water paddles and the giant steam engine that powered them were nearly deafening, there was a kind of serenity about plowing upriver at sunset, with a vast sky and emerging stars above them. They gazed at the passing landscape for a while.

"Come along," Rosebud murmured finally. "Let's find you a place to get some shut-eye." Celeste scrambled after the old hound, who methodically and patiently padded to a pile of old gunnysacks near the front of the boat. He circled a few times, and then lay down with a grunt.

"Old bones!" he sighed. He gestured to a spot

between his paws and under his one long ear, and Celeste hesitantly crawled into the warm nook.

"You'll be fine," Rosebud whispered as a grateful Celeste snuggled beneath the worn but velvet-soft ear. With the sounds of the cascading water paddles and Rosebud's heavy snoring, she fell asleep.

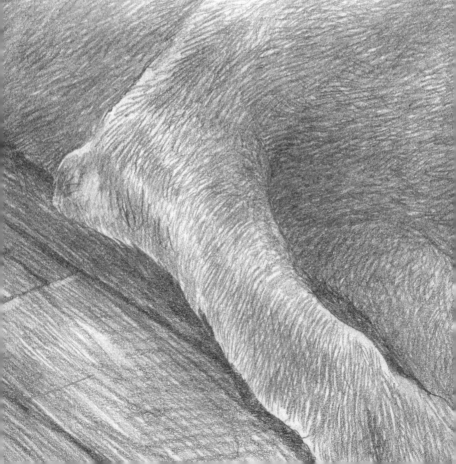

CHAPTER FOUR
Life on a Steamboat

Several times during the night, Celeste woke to the strange sounds of the men on the *Paducah Queen* guiding the steamboat through the snags and sandbars that dotted the river. From under Rosebud's ear, she caught glimpses of passing steamboats, heading in the opposite direction. The two boats would acknowledge each other with piercing, ear-numbing whistles that echoed for miles down the river. Celeste would clutch in terror at the fur on Rosebud's neck.

"It's all right," the dog whispered, after the first whistle had faded away. "They's just bein' friendly, sayin' hello to one another. You'll get used to it." The rhythm of the steam engine lulled Celeste back to sleep.

Dawn came slowly over the treetops to the east, pink and delicate. There was a slight breeze to the air, and Celeste poked her nose out from under Rosebud's protective ear. The smell of the river was everywhere, aromatic and powerful.

Rosebud woke drowsily. "Another day on the river." He yawned, shaking his head and flapping his ears and jowls with gusto. He looked out over the clay-colored water. "River's high . . . wet spring. Let's go find us some grub!"

Celeste grabbed on to his furry neck with all her strength and clung to the dog's bandanna collar. Rosebud stood up stiffly, yelping a little in pain as he stretched his three long, aged legs. They hobbled down the deck planking, Celeste still hanging in the bandanna.

"You've got spunk, I'll give you that much!" Rosebud smiled. He found an old water bucket and took a drink, and then sat heavily beside an open green door that led inside the boat housing.

"Just watch," he said to Celeste, under his breath. "Stay out of sight. Food should be arriving any minute."

Celeste stayed semiburied in Rosebud's coat, with only her nose and whiskers protruding. There were all sorts of delicious smells wafting from within the

doorway. She recognized crisp bacon and roasted cof-
fee and frying potatoes.

"Good morning, buddy," a deep voice called out,
and a man appeared at the doorjamb. He wiped
his hands on his greasy apron and smiled kindly at
Rosebud. "Here for some breakfast?"

Rosebud wagged his tail and smiled. His salmon-
colored tongue swirled around the man's fingers.

"Let's see what I got," the man said. "How about
some fatback?" He offered Rosebud an open hand dis-
playing a chunk of fatty pork, which Rosebud gulped

in a flourish of tongue and saliva.

Rosebud immediately gave a little whine, and the man smiled again. He disappeared for a moment and returned with a biscuit, plump and buttery and golden. Rosebud took it with a gulp, tail wagging.

"That's it!" The man laughed, showing his empty hands. "Go on about your lazy day." He disappeared inside.

Rosebud padded to a secluded spot between kegs and barrels and let the biscuit drop to the deck. "There you go," he said quietly to Celeste. "Breakfast. All yours . . . enjoy!"

Celeste scurried down his front leg, sniffed at the biscuit, and began her feast, suddenly realizing how hungry she was. "Thanks!" she said in between bites. "Delicious." Even though Celeste ate her fill and her hunger pangs disappeared, she hardly put a dent in the biscuit. Rosebud gobbled up the remains.

Just then, they heard a man call out from the upper

level of the boat. "Starboard she goes! Starboard!"

Rosebud turned his head to the right side of the boat. "Another snag," he grumbled. "Always the snags."

"What are they?" Celeste asked.

"Piles of trees, usually. Trees, branches, stumps . . . all kinds of whatnot that the river uproots and floats down. Could be a problem if the captain doesn't steer clear. Gotta keep your eyes open, day and night."

A bell clanged and more shouting continued back and forth as the *Paducah Queen* angled away from a mass of tangled trees. The river currents had scoured the giant sycamores and cypresses and tupelos from the shores upriver, and then slammed them one on top of another in hazardous pileups. Celeste could see that many of the tree branches and roots were below the water surface, partially hidden by the brown water and ready to rip the bottom out of the boat.

"Are we going to crash into the snag?" she asked anxiously.

"Not a chance. The captain had plenty of warning. We're keeping a good distance." He gazed up the river. "Open water ahead. We're going to make good time today."

With Celeste nestled in the bandanna, they made their way to the rear of the boat. They watched the

wooden paddles splash and circle, as the crew members threw more large chunks of wood into the fire under the boiler. The giant paddle wheel turned faster. The noise was thunderous but exhilarating. The *Paducah Queen* puffed and paddled its way up the river.

The captain, on the deck above at the wheel, blew the steam-powered whistle, adding another noise to the cacophony.

"That dang whistle!" the dog grumbled. "Enough to scare the sap out of a pine tree. Let's go sit in a shady spot for a while." He slumped back down on his pile of gunnysacks, and he and Celeste spent the rest of the day lazing in the shade, watching the steamboat crew go about their routines.

The days came and went with the same routine. Celeste, although anxious to reach St. Louis so that she could find her way back down the river on another steamboat, enjoyed Rosebud's relaxed company and gentle kindness.

"I don't know what I would have done, had it not been for you," Celeste remarked one afternoon. "I'd still be in that crate of apples, I'm sure! I'm going to miss you when I have to change steamboats."

Rosebud grinned. "Been nice to have such good company," he said. "Was gettin' kinda lonesome for me, even with all these humans. . . . Nice to have someone to talk to. And don't you worry; we'll get you back home. I know just what to do."

Evening came. Rosebud returned to the galley door for his dinner, which he again shared with his new friend. Celeste nibbled contentedly on a scrap of cheese rind and then peacefully watched evening drape across the countryside. Some boys on the crew lit iron torch baskets, filled with rags doused with oil, which hung on poles in front of the boat and dimly lit the way.

The river was dark and slow. It was a moonless night, with the stars sprinkled against the sky like silver sequins on black velvet. Celeste had never seen such an expanse of sky. It made her feel very tiny, and with a slight chill she crawled beneath Rosebud's floppy ear and drifted into a fitful sleep.

Frantic shouts woke her.

"Snag! Dead ahead! Dead ahead!"

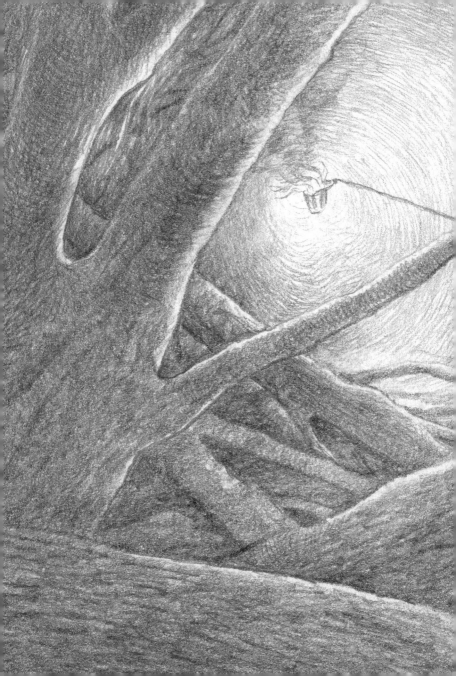

CHAPTER FIVE
Snag!

The relentless river current had slammed together hundreds of trees. The faint glow of the basket torches was barely enough to reveal the massive and treacherous mountain of trunks and branches and roots that loomed in front of them. It half floated, half dammed the river, lying like a giant dying beast. Dozens of voices called out from the engine room and the wheelhouse.

"Kill the engine!"

"Hard to port!"

"She's gonna hit!"

"Heaven preserve us!"

Celeste clung tightly to Rosebud's fur. She couldn't see the dog's kind eyes in the inky darkness, but she felt the reassurance in his voice.

"It's all right," Rosebud murmured to her. "Happens all the time. The captain will bring 'er 'round."

The crew kept hollering warnings and commands as the steamboat plowed into the mass of giant trees. With the torturous sound of splintering wood, the bow of the *Paducah* rammed into an immense sycamore. The tree tore at the wooden hull and ripped it open like a stick through a wet piece of paper. The impact jolted the boat and threw Rosebud and Celeste sideways.

With only three legs, the old dog struggled to his feet. "Somethin's mighty wrong," he growled.

Down below, the Mississippi River roared into the hull. Celeste could hear shouts and screams as men tried to battle with the onrush of water. The boat started to list as the river poured in.

"That's it!" a man called out. There was frenzy in his voice. "Every man for himself!"

The boat listed even more. Rosebud looked at Celeste. "C'mon," he said gravely. "Let's get you to a safe place." The fur on his back stood up as he painfully crouched to let Celeste cling to his bandanna. Celeste could do nothing but trust Rosebud and hang on tightly.

Rosebud limped stiffly down the deck, trying

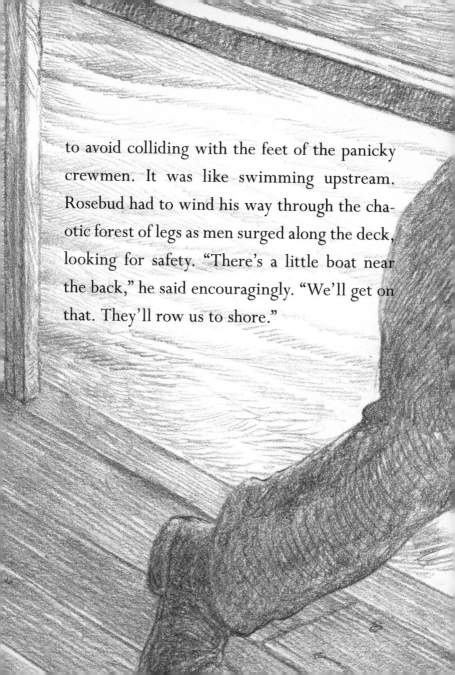

to avoid colliding with the feet of the panicky crewmen. It was like swimming upstream. Rosebud had to wind his way through the chaotic forest of legs as men surged along the deck, looking for safety. "There's a little boat near the back," he said encouragingly. "We'll get on that. They'll row us to shore."

They had almost made it to the dinghy when an enormous explosion rocked the entire boat, knocking everyone back. Rosebud was thrown against the railing with a force that knocked him down, and he sprawled onto the deck with a yelp.

"Celeste," he whined. "Something's wrong. I can't move my front legs. . . . It feels like my ribs are broken." He gave another whimper of pain. "Get into the dinghy."

"I can't leave you here," Celeste protested. She scampered around him helplessly. "Someone will see us here; they'll help you!"

"I'll be fine," the old dog insisted. "Get into the dinghy. I'll look for you when we make it back to shore."

Celeste was filled with panic. The explosion, caused by the sizzling-hot boiler hitting the cold river water, had shattered and twisted the *Paducah*, splitting

her in two. Parts of the boat littered the surface of the water, as did the men, who thrashed and screamed, some scalded by the steam, others pitched broken into the river. Their thoughts were not on saving an old hound dog.

And the dinghy was nowhere in sight.

The river continued to pour over the *Paducah Queen* and pull her down. A surge of water caught Celeste. Her eyes dark with fear, she climbed onto Rosebud's shoulder. "Rosebud!" she squeaked. "Can you try to stand up? Let's get you to something that floats."

Rosebud winced with pain between short breaths, broken ribs poking him inside. "I'll be fine," he whispered faintly. "Now you get along and climb into the dinghy." He closed his eyes. His breathing stopped, then started again.

"You must get up!" Celeste squeaked again, but another relentless wave of river water poured in. "Rosebud! Rosebud!" But there was no answer.

The water rose higher. The wreckage was sinking rapidly. With the light of the burning boat to guide her, Celeste made her way across the decking to a section of tilting wooden railing. Within jumping distance was a wooden cask, half-submerged but floating, and she hopped on. She glanced back at the deck where Rosebud lay. She thought she saw him lift his head, just as the Mississippi poured over the *Paducah Queen* and pulled it to the bottom.

CHAPTER SIX
Wreckage

Celeste clung to the cask the rest of the night. She was wet and cold, but her thoughts were of Rosebud. As pink morning light began to filter dimly through the tree-lined shore, she scanned the scene, looking for him.

Floating wreckage still littered the river surface. Celeste could see pieces of charred decking and some other casks and barrels and crates, but most of the debris was drifting south with the current. Men were out in rowboats, looking for survivors and any goods they could salvage.

Before long, some boys in a small dory spotted Celeste's cask and rowed toward her. They pulled the cask on board, not noticing the wet and shivering mouse clinging to it.

"This one says 'Flour,'" one boy said. "That makes four. We can sell this in Mariah easy."

"We're gettin' richer every minute," said another. He pointed to a wooden chair, half-submerged in the water. "Somebody'll buy that, too. Let's get it."

Celeste hid among the loot that accumulated in the little boat, finally squeezing into a wooden box of wet cigars. The boys rowed back to shore.

In the little village of
Mariah, no one spoke of anything
but the fiery explosion of the *Paducah
Queen*. The dirt street swarmed with people sell-
ing goods that had been salvaged from the wreck.
Celeste's box of cigars lay on a wooden plank along
with bottles of cherry cordial and a silk hat.

She peeked out from beneath the lid just as a tall man came to inspect the cigars. In a panic, she slipped behind the box just in time.

"How much?" the man asked. As he and the boys bickered and bartered over the cigars, Celeste nervously looked about her. Her hiding place was about to be purchased. The silk hat sat nearby, and she raced unnoticed to it, dodging underneath. Beyond that, she saw a box of sewing supplies, pins and needles and different-colored thread. It was also still damp, and the lid warped. Like a fast-moving shadow, she scurried to it and slipped inside.

It was only minutes later when a man

picked up the box. Hiding beneath packets of pins, Celeste held her breath.

"Ten cents. Not a penny more," Celeste heard the man say briskly. Then, with a stomach-surging swing, the box was flung into a wooden crate on the back of a wagon. In the darkness, Celeste felt the wagon move, and then heard the clop-clop of a horse's hooves starting down the dirt street.

The jostling and swaying of the cart continued the rest of the long day. Celeste was hungry. She poked her head out from beneath the box lid and found herself surrounded by all sorts of goods: barrels of flour, casks of molasses, crates of apples, boxes of nails. She sniffed at one of the barrels at the back of the wagon, found a tiny crevasse, and squeezed inside.

The barrel was filled with cornmeal. Celeste rolled down into the pale yellow meal and gratefully stuffed her tummy with it, finally burrowing into it to sleep.

She awoke to the sound of the horse harness jingling. Another day of traveling followed. Feeling brave, she climbed up on top of the meal barrel and watched the countryside pass by. Tall oaks and hickories surrounded the tiny road, which was little more

than a path cutting through the woods, crowded with ferns. Instead of the nearly flat, sandy terrain she was used to at Oakley, the land here was rolling, the road full of rocks and ruts. There was a ruggedness to it, and a sharpness to the air.

The horse trudged steadily along as the harness jingled in rhythm. Suddenly, it reared up on its hind legs and let out a bloodcurdling whinny. Its eyes were white with fear as it reared again, tipping the little wagon and the cornmeal crate with it. Celeste gripped the wooden lid tightly.

"Whoa!" the driver cried out. "Steady . . . steady . . ." He glanced at the ground and discovered the culprit: a sizable timber rattler was coiled in the middle of the road, ready to strike. It took up most of the trail; there was no going around it.

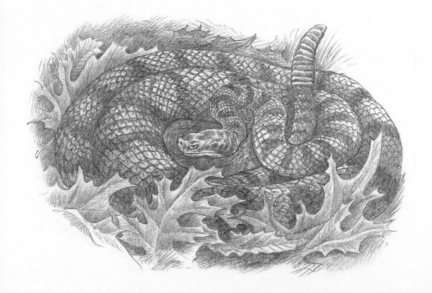

"Steady! Steady!" the driver repeated calmly, and pulled back on the reins. The terrified horse would have none of it and, with another shriek, reared again, this time knocking into the front of the wagon with a jolt. The cornmeal barrel teetered for a moment on the rear edge of the wagon, and then fell with a thud to the ground. Celeste landed alongside, sliding through the avalanche of cornmeal.

The wagon wheels threatened to roll over her as the driver eased the wagon back. Celeste shook the cornmeal off of her whiskers and dashed into a nearby path of ferns.

She watched as the driver climbed down from the wagon with his rifle and shot the rattlesnake. The snake twisted and writhed for a moment, then lay still.

The man walked around the wagon and saw the overturned barrel of meal. "Humph," he mumbled to himself, scraping what cornmeal he could back into the barrel and shoving it safely back on the wagon.

He mounted the wagon seat again. "H'yah!" he

called out, and the nervous horse started back down the trail.

"Wait!" Celeste squeaked back. "Wait for me!"

But the wagon creaked down the trail through the woods and disappeared.

Celeste was once again alone.

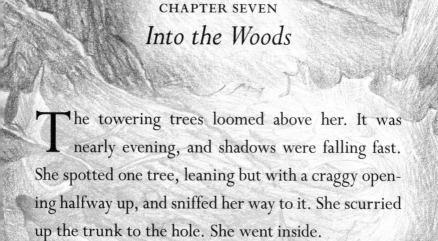

CHAPTER SEVEN
Into the Woods

The towering trees loomed above her. It was nearly evening, and shadows were falling fast. She spotted one tree, leaning but with a craggy opening halfway up, and sniffed her way to it. She scurried up the trunk to the hole. She went inside.

It was dark, of course. After her home in the attic, it seemed rough and cold, but it was protective and secure, and Celeste was eager to have a safe spot for the night. There were dry leaves and some soft mosses padding the little space, making it a bit inviting. There was even a little pile of acorns and beechnuts, and Celeste nibbled at one. She curled herself into a ball under some oak leaves and tried to get warm.

Her dark brown eyes widened as she heard a scratching, skittering sound outside the hole, and then a large gray-brown head poked inside.

"What the blazes are *you* doin' here?" demanded a gray squirrel. "You get out of here this instant! Chester! Come quick! A *thief*!"

"I . . . I," Celeste began, but the one squirrel's face was instantly replaced by another, Chester's whiskers twitching in annoyance.

"A mouse!" he exclaimed. "How about *that*? You

jus' come on in, easy as you please, and make yourself at home like ya *own* the place!"

Celeste was just about to speak when the first squirrel's head appeared again.

"Like ya *own* the place!" she screeched.

Chester returned. "Such *nerve*!"

Hazel poked her head in. "Robbin' us blind, I'll bet."

Then Chester was back again. "Who is she?" he barked.

Hazel returned and stared at Celeste. "Heck if I know. Never laid eyes on her before."

Celeste finally found her voice. "I'm sorry," she said. "I didn't realize this was someone's home. I was just trying to find a spot to spend the night. You see, there was this snake on the road, and the cornme—"

"Somebody's *home*?" Chester interrupted. "This ain't nobody's home. It's hardly big enough for storing stuff." His head disappeared for a moment and Celeste heard him outside the hole. "She said 'home.'"

He giggled. "Can you believe that one?" They both giggled some more.

Hazel's head appeared. "Enough, little mousey. You're bein' evicted. This is *our* territory. And you touch just one of those nuts and your name is *mud*. Get it?"

"Y-yes, I understand," Celeste stuttered. Everything had happened so quickly, she hardly knew how to react to the pair of squirrels. This wasn't exactly the hospitality she was used to. And it was nearly dark.

She crawled out of the little opening and began to make her way down the tree trunk to the ground. Her tail drooped and her whiskers quivered in the chill of the evening air.

The two squirrels watched her climb down. "Uh . . . hey . . . you," Chester said. "Hold on. I guess you can stay *one* night here. Right, Hazel?"

Hazel nodded. "One night. Just because it's late."

"Thanks!" Celeste squeaked gratefully. "One night would be wonderful. I'm very tired." She scrambled back up the rough bark of the hickory. "My name is Celeste," she said, extending a paw.

Hazel grinned. She grabbed Celeste's paw and shook it hard. "Pleasure," she replied. "Welcome to Chestnut Holler. This here's Chester. Where ya hail from, Celeste? Not from around here, I'm bettin'. You got that highfalutin way about ya."

"I don't mean to be . . . highfalutin," Celeste stammered. "I came up the river on a steamboat. I live at Oakley. It's very far from here. I'm trying to figure out how to get back."

"Well, how the heck did you make it here?" Chester

asked. Celeste told them the story of the cotton wagon, and the steamboat disaster, and of dear Rosebud, and the rattlesnake. When she ended, the two squirrels sat in silence, dumbfounded.

"Law's a-mercy," Chester sighed finally. He looked at Celeste kindly. "Little gal, you can stay here in our storage nook jus' as long as you like, y'hear?"

Hazel chimed in. "My, yes. No need to look anywhere else for a place to stay. Our nook is your nook, y'hear?"

Celeste smiled as her two new hosts began making a fuss, offering to add dry leaves and fresh acorns. "Thank you, really," she said. "I'll be fine." She crawled back into the coziest part of the nook and curled up.

Chester grinned as he watched Celeste fall asleep. "Bring up some of those dried hay-scented ferns, Hazel," he whispered. "They'll be nice and toasty on a chilly night, and smell good, too." Hazel gathered some of the ferns, and the two squirrels tucked them around Celeste, who was already deeply asleep. Then they scurried back to their leaf nest, high in a neighboring white pine. Night was just settling in; the crickets were already singing.

CHAPTER EIGHT
New Friends

H ello? Hello!"
Celeste awoke to a patch of sun hitting the oak leaves that surrounded her, and the loud chatter of the pair of squirrels, who took turns looking in at her.

"Good mornin'!" Hazel scritched. "We have breakfast for you!" She dropped several maple seeds into the nook, and then Chester chimed in. "Good

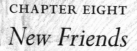

mornin'! Better get up!" he called cheerily.

"G-good morning," Celeste said with a stretch. "It must be late. . . . The sun says I've slept a long time!"

"Yes indeedy, you have. Now it's time to rise and shine," Chester said. The two squirrels scooted down the tree with ease and onto the forest floor.

Celeste quickly stroked her whiskers and licked her paws. She took a good look around.

The trees above her head were tinged with colors: the poplars and hickories golden yellow, the maples scarlet red, the oaks dusty purple, and the chestnuts mustard brown. And there was a chill; the air seemed clearer, details seemed more vivid, and every leaf and twig distinct.

Hazel and Chester waved from the base of an immense white pine tree that stood nearby. "Over here!" Hazel called out, waving. There were several other mice gathered around the roots of the pine, and two fat beavers, their brown fur slicked back and shiny.

Celeste greeted the small crowd with a smile. "Well . . . hello!" she said.

"These are just some of the folks around that wanted to . . . meet you," offered Chester.

"A kind of welcomin' committee," added Hazel. Her eyes flashed with excitement.

"Thank you," Celeste said uneasily. "I . . . I appreciate the welcome."

"Where ya from?" asked one of the mice.

"Why ya here?" asked another.

One of the beavers lumbered over and peered down at Celeste. "You're a pretty little thing. You ain't from around here, are ya?" he asked.

"Forest," Chester admonished. "You're scarin' her. Give her some breathin' room. I told you all her story. Now just let her get accustomed to all of us."

The other beaver smiled, and extended her paw. "I'm Chloe," she said.

Celeste smiled appreciatively at Chloe. "I'm from south of here, a long way south," she answered, her tail wiggling with apprehension. "I . . . I'm here because . . . because of the way things happen sometimes."

One of the mice chortled. "Huh?" he blurted out. "What kinda answer is that?"

"I just mean that I started out days and days ago getting some dinner, and I ended up far from home. I hardly know what to say."

A deer mouse with half his tail missing spoke up.

"You don't sound like any mouse I've met before," he said.

"Hesh up, Monroe," admonished Hazel. "That any way to speak friendly to a stranger?"

"Sorry," the mouse replied sheepishly. "Didn't

mean any disrespect. Just hadn't heard anybody talk that way before, is all."

"I guess I do speak differently," offered Celeste. "Just like you sound different to me."

The deer mouse shrugged, looking embarrassed.

Peeved, Hazel stamped her foot. "You folks need to understand," she said. "This poor gal has been on quite an adventure! She's seen things we can't even begin to imagine!"

Chester flicked his tail vigorously and spoke up. "Yes! Tell us again about the big human house!" he exclaimed. "And the steamboat!" The others started chattering excitedly, the mice squeaking excitedly and the beavers slapping their tails.

"Was there real fancy china in the big house?" someone asked.

"What kind of foods did you eat?" asked another.

"What's a steamboat, exactly?" asked a third.

"Tell us again about Lafayette, and bein' up in the

air!" The questions came hard and fast, and Celeste tried to answer them all.

"You've seen a lot," Chester said finally. "You plannin' on settlin' here? Stayin' on with us?" The little group quieted down and looked at Celeste expectantly.

Celeste grew pensive. She hadn't had a moment to think about her future. Heading back toward Oakley seemed daunting; she didn't even know where she was, or the first thing about getting back. How would she ever get back to the river, and on the right boat heading down south? And if she did, how would she know where to get off the boat? The questions seemed unanswerable and endless. She studied the little group of squirrels and mice. She made a decision.

"I . . . I guess I'd like to stay here until I figure out how to get back home," she said. "That is, if you'll have me."

"Why, of course we'll have you!" said Hazel warmly. "You just consider yourself a part of our family."

The others squeaked and chattered their agreement, and Celeste felt the tips of her ears redden with pleasure and gratitude.

"Thank you," she said simply.

CHAPTER NINE
Living Dangerously

Celeste spent the days getting to know her new friends and trying to get accustomed to living in the woods. Everything was a change for her. Back at Oakley Plantation, there had been a seemingly endless supply of food scraps from the human table. And there had been Joseph, the kind boy who'd given her peanuts or pecans and a warm shirt pocket to nestle in.

But here the nights were filled with strange sounds: grunts of black bears, yipping of red foxes, and hoots of gray owls. The foxes were especially chilling; Monroe told her repeatedly of his near escape from a fox, and the way he'd ended up with half his tail bitten off.

"Oh, yes," he told her gravely. "They jump on you, foxes do, comin' from out of nowhere. Before you even know what's happened. So stay sharp, and keep your eyes open for foxes. Yes indeed!"

Celeste would gulp. Oakley, even with its house cat, had seemed warm and safe. She was glad she had her newly made friends to warn her of dangers in the woods.

One evening they sat together beneath Hazel and Chester's giant white pine. Celeste, wide-eyed, listened as they all whispered their astonishing stories. Monroe had just told them once again of his escape from the fox. Pawpaw gave an account of her near-fatal brush with a broad-winged hawk. Chester told of his near miss many times with the spray of gunshot.

Hazel looked seriously at Celeste. "Danger everywhere, dear," she said. "Mark my words."

"Keep alert!" warned Chester.

"Danger everywhere!" repeated Hazel.

Forest looked at the little group and sighed. "Well, there's danger, and then there's *danger*," he said soberly. They all looked curiously at the old beaver.

"See this coat?" he continued, running a paw through his thick, silky fur. Everyone nodded in admiration. "Yep, it's pretty wonderful. Keeps me warm, keeps me dry. Proud of my coat. Problem is, humans think it's wonderful, too. Nearly everyone in my family is gone now. All because of this coat. From what I hear, they all ended up as hats. Hats! Can you imagine that! Their coats end up sittin' on top of a human's head. And the human is happy and proud. But I've got no family left!"

"It's just me and Forest," Chloe added. "Used to be my kin, and Forest's kin, all around these parts. Hundreds of us! We're the only ones left. Forest is right. All our family ended up as hats."

"They came, the humans did, with traps made with sharp teeth. Caught us in the traps. Sometimes the traps were underwater, and we would drown. They'd come and take us away. I never knew what happened."

"Then one day we saw it," Chloe said.

"Saw what?" Celeste asked.

"Well, one day we was in the woods, next to the pathway the humans travel on with their wagons. And, mind you, it was daytime. We used to go out and work in the daytime. Not anymore! Now we only work in the nighttime. Well, a wagon went by, plain as day . . ." Chloe stopped speaking, her voice faltering.

"Let me tell it," Forest said. "A wagon went by, plain as day. And it was filled with pelts. My family. The skins were stacked, one on top of th'other. Tied up in bundles. If I hadn't seen it my own self, I never would have believed it."

Everyone sat silently, contemplating the beavers' story.

"My ma, my pa, all my kin," Forest said quietly. "Never saw 'em again."

Celeste thought back to her friend Joseph. His gentle kindness seemed like a dream. She missed the safety of his home and the comfort of his voice.

"They can't be all as bad as you say," she said. "The human who took me into his home and cared for me was a good human. He gave me plenty of foo—"

"They're all bad!" Chester interrupted. "They cannot be trusted. You must stay away from them, no matter what."

"He's right," Chloe agreed. "Keep away. If you had seen that wagon . . ." Her voice trailed off.

Pawpaw was shivering, his dark brown eyes wide and anxious. "See what you've done? You've upset Pawpaw," Hazel said sharply. "All this storytellin' . . . It ain't no way to make Celeste feel at home, now, is it? Let's all get safely back to our homes. Good night, everyone. Celeste, I apologize for the crazy way these folks were talkin' this evening."

"That's all right, Hazel. The stories were . . . interesting. I probably needed to hear them. I need to know what's out there."

Night was falling, and the little party broke up. Celeste scurried quickly back to her hollow nook. The fur on her back was standing straight up.

CHAPTER TEN
Beaver Dam Adventure

Very, very early one morning, just before dawn, Celeste scurried from her little nook and wandered down to the stream nearby. She followed it along until she came to the expanse of water that was Forest and Chloe's domain. Their dam across the small creek had created a serene, clear pond. Crayfish and snails, minnows and chubs, herons and kingfishers had all discovered the new wetland and had made themselves at home.

She scrambled up one end of the dam. The seemingly jumbled and haphazard assembly of sticks and branches was actually a well-planned design. Surprisingly strong and durable, it was capable of surviving spring floods, and even the occasional trampling of a stray bear charging through.

Celeste perched at the top of the chewed end of a branch and surveyed the scene from the tall vantage point. The pond was dark and peaceful. The edges of it were slowly creeping all through the surrounding woods, inch by inch, as water from the small creek backed up and got deeper and deeper. A few of the trees were dead, their roots waterlogged. Woodpecker holes dotted their trunks and branches. Other trees were facing the same fate.

"Well, look who's here," Forest exclaimed when he saw Celeste perched on top of the branch.

Chloe's head immediately bobbed up from the smooth surface of the pond. "Celeste, dear! Good

morning," she called out cheerily. "What brings you here so bright and early? You here to help us with the dam?" She made a sharp V in the water as she paddled up to the dam.

Celeste smiled. "I doubt I'd be much help, but I'd be happy to try," she said. "I'm not sure what I'd do."

"I'm just foolin' with you, dear," Chloe replied. "Dam buildin' is hard work. Takes strong teeth and jaws. You just ain't built for it."

"I'm not even sure why you want to build one in the first place," Celeste said.

Forest stood upright.

"Safety!" he snorted. "Just try and see a fox getting into our lodge. Or a hawk. Ha! It's a place to live. We can build a dam and make a pond and then build our lodge." He gestured to a mound of sticks in the middle of the pond. "See that? Home."

"I see a little hill," Celeste said. "I don't see a home."

"That's it. Snug and warm and dry inside."

"How do you get . . . inside?"

"Entrance is under the water. You swim into it."

Celeste was intrigued. A home in the middle of the water. Forest and Chloe had ingeniously constructed a dam, which had created a spot for them to build their unique home. "May I see inside?" she asked.

"Well, now, there's a problem," Forest replied. He sat upright, puffing out his chest, then took a deep breath. Celeste watched as he sat, without breathing, minute after minute. Just as she was about to panic, the beaver breathed out again.

"See? Chloe and me, we can hold our breath," he said.

"That was really something," Celeste said, amazed.

"That was nothin'. I can go much longer. How about you?"

Celeste took a deep breath and held it for as long as she could. Her tiny lungs could only hold so much air. In just a few seconds, she was gasping.

"Not so good," Chloe remarked. She pointed across the pond to the lodge. "You'd need a lot more breath than that." She looked at Forest, who was deep in thought. "He's getting an idea," she said quietly. "See the quivering nose and stony expression? He always looks that way when he's about to get an idea."

"Got it!" Forest chattered suddenly, slapping his tail. "Chloe, you know that turtle shell over by the edge of the pond? You found it yesterday."

"Yep, know the one. I'll go fetch it."

"This just might work," Forest continued. "You'll have to be brave, Celeste. Trust us. We'll take you for a ride and show you around the pond. You'll even see the inside of the lodge."

It didn't take long for Forest and Chloe to rig a tiny diving chamber for Celeste using the turtle shell and sticks. Two sticks under the shell served as a small platform, with the shell trapping the air. Forest dragged it to the edge of the pond.

"Ready?" he asked.

"I think so," Celeste replied hesitantly. "Are you sure it's safe?"

"If Forest built it, it's safe," Chloe replied. "Hang on, dearie!"

Celeste climbed onto the frame of the underwater contraption, and Forest and Chloe each took a side, grabbing on to the stick framework. Then they guided it into the cool water.

They paddled out. Celeste watched as the water passed beneath her paws, dark and deep. The tips of her toes got wet, but otherwise she was dry and protected. There was plenty of air trapped inside the dome of the shell.

"All right in there?" she heard Forest shout.

"Yes, I'm fine!" Celeste answered back. "It's dark, but I'm fine!"

A minute later, she heard Chloe's voice. "Hang on, now, Celeste. Good and tight," she said seriously. "We're going under!"

Celeste felt the turtle shell contraption dip down-
ward, and she could tell she was going down, down,
down into the water. It got much darker inside, pitch-
black. She felt her heart race, and her breaths came
faster and faster.

She frantically scrambled from one side of the
sticks to the other. "I . . . I . . . !" she stuttered, but
she was too frightened to speak.

Suddenly, with a swoosh, the shell emerged from the water and up into a dark, wet room. Celeste felt with her paws and found herself on top of a floor made of sticks and cattail leaves, mixed with mud. She crawled out from under the shell, and her eyes adjusted to the dark.

The ceiling was domed. The air was damp and smelled of mud, but the lodge was well engineered and warm. The dark shapes of Forest and Chloe loomed over her.

"Well, you made it. What do you think?" asked Forest.

"I told you he was smart," Chloe said proudly. "Imagine riding in a turtle shell underwater!"

Celeste was still trying to adjust to the dark of the lodge. "That was . . . an adventure," she said. "We're in the lodge? We went all the way under the pond?"

"Yes indeedy, we did, Miss Celeste."

"It's very . . . dark. But very cozy!"

"This is where we shake the water off before we head into the living area," Chloe said. "We want to keep that part nice and dry, where we'll spend the winter, and raise a family next year."

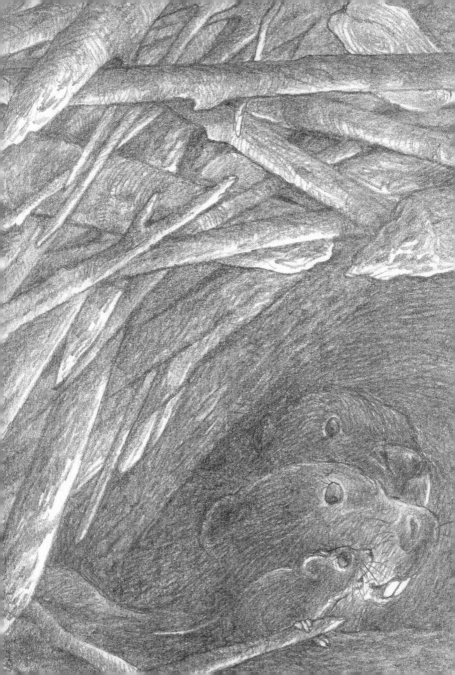

Celeste had heard mention of winter. "Spend the winter?" she asked.

"Yep. Lots of folks go to sleep for months. We'll be out and about, weather permittin'. Step in here."

Celeste was still unsure of what she meant, and how anyone could sleep that long, but Chloe wanted to show her around the lodge. They entered a second small chamber.

"And in here will be the babies' nursery," she commented, "and over here we store some extra-good roots and bulbs, really tasty things."

Forest tapped the side of the den. "See? Strong! The outside is layered with mud, hard as stone. I defy a wolf to get through it!"

"And, of course, the underwater entrance makes for good protection . . . and so cozy!" Chloe added.

Celeste sighed contentedly. "I can see why you like living here so much."

Forest slapped his tail with pleasure. "How 'bout another ride? We'll take you on a different kind of spin this time."

Celeste crawled back under the shell and again

they traveled underwater, emerging in the middle of the pond, some distance from the lodge. Celeste could tell they were at the surface again.

"Hang on!" she heard Forest yell. "Hang on tight!"

With a sudden jerk, the whole turtle shell upended. Celeste still clung to the sticks inside. In a moment she was in the open air; the turtle shell was now a boat, and she was being pulled across the tranquil surface of the pond.

"This is more like it!" she squealed. "Wheee!"

They sailed around the pond for part of the morning, until Chloe and Forest decided it was time to get back to work. "The dam won't get built by itself!" Chloe said. "Celeste, off you go. See you soon."

Celeste looked gratefully at the two beavers, their fur wet and glistening. "Thank you," she said. "What a

wonderful, exciting morning." Then she hopped from the turtle shell craft onto the muddy shore of the pond, and scurried back to her nook in the tree.

CHAPTER ELEVEN

Tree House Home

W ake up!" came a voice, and Celeste awoke. Hazel's face appeared. "Time's a-wastin'!"

"Wh-what's the matter?" Celeste asked groggily.

In a flash, Hazel was gone and Chester's face appeared. "Not a thing, Miss Celeste," he said cheerfully. "We . . . Hazel and myself . . . we're invitin' you to visit our nest today, that's all. Just extending a little bit of Chestnut Holler hospitality. We heard that Forest and Chloe showed you their place, and now we want to do the same."

Celeste knew the squirrels had a nest in what had to be the tallest tree in the woods, a towering white pine that rose above the rest of the trees like a sentinel. And from what she had heard, their nest was near the very top.

"I . . . I don't know," she said doubtfully. "I appreciate the invitation, but I'm not much of a tree climber."

"Don't matter at all how you climb," Hazel said. "You just hang on to us tight."

Chester said, "And don't look down!" He giggled.

Celeste reluctantly followed them across the leaf litter to the base of the giant pine. She looked up; the huge trunk seemed like a mountain. The branches, far above the woods floor, stretched up and up, looking like a green cloud.

Celeste gulped. "I think that may be a little too high up for me," she murmured.

"That's crazy talk," Chester chittered.

"Crazy talk!" Hazel agreed. "You just hop on my back. You'll be up there in our pine tree before you can say 'walnut.'"

Celeste gulped again but climbed onto Hazel's strong back. Hazel flicked her bushy tail in excitement, tickling Celeste's nose and causing her to sneeze. "Sorry," Hazel said. "Hang on, here we go!"

In a flash, they were off, with Chester and Hazel scrambling wildly around the tree, corkscrew fashion, spiraling their way up the enormous tree trunk. Celeste clung to Hazel's back, scarcely daring to breathe, digging her tiny claws into the thick fur.

The ground quickly became a distant backdrop.

They reached the first, lower branches of the pine, and Hazel stopped to rest. "Your turn," she said to Chester, and Celeste hopped onto Chester's back for the rest of the trip. They leaped from branch to branch, scurrying between the massive trunk and the ladder-like limbs that took them higher and higher.

At last they reached the nest. Celeste carefully hopped onto a branch and looked around. She was a little dizzy; the ground was far, far below. A breeze swept through the pine needles, making a hushed whir that sounded magical, and gently rocked the tree. It felt like another world, a private one.

Celeste had a thought, and she looked out across the tops of the tree canopy, hoping for perhaps a glimpse of Lafayette flapping and gliding across in the distance. Her heart sank a bit, as she saw no familiar silhouette of her osprey friend.

A series of limbs jutted out from the trunk. At the crotch of the trunk and one of the branches was a well-constructed lodge of sticks and dry leaves. Everything was so tucked and fitted together with such care that Celeste doubted even a very strong wind could blow it away.

"Well, here we are," Hazel said. She gestured to an opening near the base of the leaf nest, where some leaves formed a sort of flap. "Right through

here." In a flash, she had slipped into the nest and disappeared.

"After you," said Chester. Celeste poked her nose
into the leaf opening and burrowed in.

It was small, and a little cramped, but spacious
enough for two squirrels. The leaves and sticks formed
a tight, compact chamber, lined with soft mosses and
fur. Celeste noticed many nuts jammed here and
there.

They all climbed over one another in order to
find room to sit, and they laughed as somebody's paw
landed on somebody else's face.

"So cozy," Celeste sighed finally. "I'm so happy to
have seen this. You have a wonderful tree house."

"Our home is your home," chittered Chester
warmly.

Celeste smiled. "Yes, it *is* a home," she said.

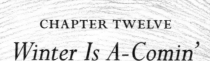

CHAPTER TWELVE
Winter Is A-Comin'

There was something melancholy to the air. Celeste felt it but couldn't explain it. She thought wistfully of Oakley. Everything in Chestnut Holler was new and different; she had pangs for her old attic home, and missed Lafayette and Violet. Her new friends had been lifesavers, and they cared for her and included her. But there seemed to be something missing.

The sun was like a dwindling fire, with every day a bit shorter than the last. The air had a crisp quality to it that was new to Celeste.

There was lots of activity in the hollow, but none of it made sense to Celeste. Hazel and Chester spent the days frantically gathering nuts. She watched them digging holes in the ground, burying walnuts and chestnuts and acorns by the hundreds, cover them up with dirt and dead leaves, then looking suspiciously around, as though expecting marauding invaders to steal their booty.

And Monroe and Pawpaw and Hunter were busy doing the same with seeds and pine nuts. She hardly saw them. Their tiny nest in the knothole of an old rotting stump was stuffed with dried grasses and ferns; a larder of seeds and nuts was bursting at the seams.

Forest and Chloe were across the meadow, constantly adding to their lodge and to the dam that crossed the small creek. What before had been a trickling stream and a small pond was now a shimmering wetland. A cheerful pair of wood ducks was there nearly every day, excited at the expanse of water and new habitat.

And the nuts! They fell from the sky. The sprawling, towering chestnut trees dominated the woods, and the spiny husks of their nuts seemed to carpet the ground. They poked up among the brightly colored fallen leaves, like sea urchins among corals. It seemed to rain beechnuts, and both the scarlet and white oaks produced an unimaginable number of acorns. It was a very bountiful fall.

Armies of wild turkeys passed by Celeste as they foraged. With stately demeanor, they strolled by, eating chestnut after chestnut and acorn after acorn, happily clucking to one another, stuffing themselves so that their crops nearly burst.

The trees were alive with birds, too. They filled the branches, calling to one another and moving through the woods canopy in waves. Some were so tiny, they were invisible high in the treetops; Celeste just heard their chirps and calls up among the colorful leaves.

Celeste searched under the leaf litter for another delicious nut. The hickory nuts had shells as hard as iron; she preferred the softer beechnuts. As she savored the flavorful meat, she heard a voice from a low branch overhead.

"Hey!" it chirped.

Celeste looked up. A small bird, hardly any bigger than herself, darted among the twigs. It repeatedly glanced down at Celeste as it poked about the golden-orange beech leaves. Its feathers were dull yellow and gray, but it had bright black eyes. It never seemed to sit still.

"Hey to you," Celeste answered back.

The warbler dipped its wings and flitted down to the ground, landing beside Celeste with a flourish. "I'm Silas," said the bird. He darted his head and snatched a tiny worm from the ground. "Eating like a maniac. Can't seem to get enough."

Celeste smiled. "I'm Celeste."

"You should be fatter by now," Silas remarked.

"I beg your pardon?"

"You're not fat enough! You'll have a hard time getting through the winter the way you are."

"Winter?"

"Sure! Of course, I won't be here. . . . I'll be long gone. But any folks sticking around these parts are going to need a layer of fat if they're going to survive."

"Really?" Celeste didn't know what to say.

"Look, eat all you can. You'll be grateful for the advice when the snow covers everything. I've heard all about it."

"Snow? What is snow?" asked Celeste.

"You've got a lot to learn, sweetheart!" the warbler chuckled grimly. He looked up as a group of other warblers quickly made their way through the branches overhead. They'd soon be gone. "You'll find out. Gotta go!"

Celeste sat, puzzled. Snow? No one had mentioned snow to her. She decided to ask Hazel about it, and scampered off in the direction of the big pine.

Hazel was busily digging a hole next to a stump, her mouth full with a large walnut. "Hthwth athwatha," she mumbled over the large nut.

"Hazel, I need to know what 'snow' is. Can you tell me?" Celeste asked.

Hazel spit the nut out into the freshly dug hole. "Snow? Of course! Don't ya know?"

"Never heard of it. I have no idea."

"Snow. Cold. White. Comes from the sky. Snow means winter is here."

"Is it something I should be worried about?"

Hazel looked at Celeste with a mixture of concern and disbelief. "Dearie, if you don't know what snow is, then you should be worried! Snow makes for tough livin'. You need to pre*pare*. I guess we all jus' figgered you knew what it was. To tell you the truth, we was all wonderin' why you were lollygaggin' around!"

"But prepare for what?"

"For the *cold*. For no *food*. For wind that howls through the trees with no leaves to stop it. For snowdrifts that nearly cover the trees. For nights so long you'll forget what the sun looks like. And this all lasts for months and months! *That's* what!" The squirrel had a dark look in her eyes. "You'll need to store up as much food as you can. Ya know how all the trees have given us a passel of nuts this year? That's just the forest lookin' out for us. The forest knows this is gonna be a tough winter."

She looked intently at Celeste, and realized it was almost too much for the little mouse to take in. "Look," she said. "Winter is a-comin'. We all knew it would. Thought you did, too. You've maybe got enough time to haul some nuts into the nook, store some food, and try to make it through." She paused. "We'll try to help ya, best we can."

Celeste could do nothing but stare blankly at Hazel. As if on cue, a little breeze sifted through the trees, chilly and sobering. Celeste felt the chill pass

all the way through to the tip of her tail.

She began a frantic search-and-gather effort, bringing as many nuts and seeds as she could find into her nook in the hickory tree. It was very hard work; the nook was a good distance up the tree trunk, and Celeste was only just a little bigger than the nuts she struggled to collect. As she worked, she began to realize how easy her life had been at Oakley; yes, there had been cats and people, but the people had supplied an endless variety of food, and it was there for the taking. And there was no snow at Oakley.

She worked and worked. At the end of one day, she had successfully accumulated exactly seven beechnuts, four acorns, and one chestnut, and a small cache of weed seeds. It wasn't nearly enough, not for months and months, like Hazel had said.

She set out again, starting her way back down the

hickory on another foray into the woods. There was a noise below, and she paused to listen.

Human footsteps made a rustling, swooshing sound through the leaves.

She saw a human boy below.

CHAPTER THIRTEEN

Boy with an Ax

The boy came ambling through the woods, carrying an ax. Suddenly, he stopped directly below Celeste and stood for a moment, contemplating the hickory.

He stepped back, spitting on his hands. Then he swung the ax over his shoulder and, with a sudden, powerful move, aimed the heavy ax at the tree. The blade sliced through the air, striking the hickory with a loud thwack!

The tree shuddered and Celeste nearly fell off, and she scurried quickly into her nook.

A moment later came another thwack, then another, and another. Celeste's whole body quivered as the blows vibrated through the tough hickory wood.

It wasn't long before she heard a cracking sound, and she felt the tree groan and shake. "Oh!" she squeaked a moment later as the tree suddenly fell to the woods floor with a loud crash.

Celeste hit the wall of the nook hard, and she squeaked with shock. More blows of the ax came, closer and closer, as the tree was chopped into short lengths. Celeste froze, hoping the ax blows would

stop, but suddenly the ax blade sliced into her little nook, splitting it open and exposing Celeste. She was covered with nuts and leaves and dusty wood chips.

She looked up, trembling.

"Well, hello," a voice said. "I'm afraid I just made you homeless."

Celeste looked up into the dark eyes of the young man with the ax. His black hair was long and rather dirty, curled in some places, straight in others. He smelled strongly of wood smoke.

He was barefoot. He had long limbs: he seemed to be nearly all arms and legs. His sleeves were too short, as were the legs of his pants, as though he had outgrown them. They had been torn and patched, and made from homespun material dyed with indigo and walnuts. He was no longer a child, but then again seemed too young to be chopping trees in the woods.

It was his eyes that caught Celeste by the heart. They were deep and thoughtful, but they also had a twinkle that hinted at a humorous side. They looked right into Celeste's eyes, just the way that Joseph's had. She felt glad inside.

He put out his hand, slowly, gently. Celeste recognized the gesture and crawled in without hesitation.

"Well!" the boy said, laughing a little. "You're a brave mouse!"

With light fingers, he delicately brushed the bits of splintered wood and dried leaves off of Celeste's face and whiskers, and stroked her between her ears, just as Joseph had done.

"It seems I've just chopped down your home. Now, it'd be a shame to leave you here with nothin'." He chuckled. "So how about you comin' with me?"

He hung his outer vest on a tree branch and put Celeste in its pocket. Celeste burrowed down inside and then poked her head back out, just as she had dozens of times in Joseph's shirt.

The boy laughed out loud.

"Make yourself at home!" he said, picking the ax
up and finishing what he had started, chopping the
hickory into lengths for firewood. "Seems only fair!"

Celeste watched him as he swung the ax grace-
fully but powerfully, hitting the right spot on the tree
each time, reducing the tree to firewood with ease.

He finally finished the work and, sweaty but satisfied, gathered pieces of the wood in his sinewy arms. He was lean, but the load he carried indicated the strength. He started to walk away, then turned and smiled, remembering the vest, and Celeste. He carefully draped the vest with its precious cargo over the logs and started walking back through the woods.

Celeste looked up at the towering white pine overhead. She saw Hazel and Chester staring down at her, eyes wide in amazement.

CHAPTER FOURTEEN
Log Cabin

They walked down a slope, passing over a small spring. Celeste could smell wood smoke in the air, and sensed they were near the boy's home. Sure enough, a small cabin appeared in a clearing, with a stone chimney out of which poured curly wisps of smoke.

It was not the fine home that Oakley had been, with its many glass-paned windows and deep porches. This home was hardly bigger than Oakley's hen-house; it had no windows, except for one small one on one side, with a wooden shutter instead of glass panes. There was one door, with hinges made of leather pieces.

The walls of the cabin were made of rough-hewn logs, most of which still had their bark attached. The logs were chinked with wattle and daub, a mixture of wet clay and grass, in an effort to keep out the weather. The roof was oak shingle. The cabin was modest, but what it lacked in size and grandeur it made up for in sturdy construction.

A woman sat out in back of the cabin, wearing a faded dress that was a bit frayed at the hem. She wore a gray wool shawl. She was humming a tune as she methodically plucked the feathers from a chicken and stuffed them into a sack. She glanced up as the boy approached and smiled.

"Good! Needed some wood," she called out, continuing her work. "Set it down inside."

"Yes, Mama."

Celeste watched with interest from the vest pocket as the boy pushed aside the door and laid the firewood on the stone hearth. She saw a snug, neatly kept room, clean but spare. The floor was made of planks of wood, well scrubbed. There was a large breakfront, with glass doors, and a crystal oil lamp, and pair

of wing chairs with needlepoint cushions, but the rest of the room was sparse. There were a few nice china pieces, but most of the dishes were mismatched, chipped, or made of tin. There was no decoration on the walls, except for a small mirror. The room smelled of wood smoke and cured meats.

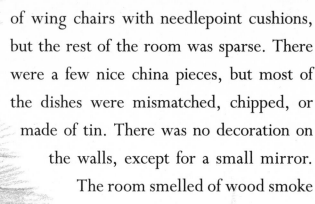

The boy scooped Celeste into his hands and held her up. "You aren't much afraid, are you?" he whispered. Celeste looked into his eyes. The kindness that lay behind them was calming, and she didn't struggle or even wiggle. She looked up at him and sniffed. The boy laughed and slipped her back into his vest pocket.

He climbed a series of wooden rungs that had been pegged into the wall. Tucked under the eaves of the roof was a bed pallet, narrow and neat, so close to the roof that he had to tuck his head to get there.

"This'll be your little hideaway," he whispered to Celeste. "Just you and me and my brother and sisters, but they won't bother you none." He sprawled on the corn-husk pallet and let Celeste nose around the bed.

"White whiskers, white as snow," he said. "And those big brown eyes. There's a quickness to you, mouse, but a sadness, too. Like me sometimes," the boy added quietly. "Ma would have liked you. She was my first ma, but she passed on 'cause of the milk fever. Then Pa married my mama." He looked very thoughtful. "Guess I got lucky."

Just then they heard the clang of an iron kettle and

Mama's voice at the fireplace below.

"Elizabeth, put the milk pitcher on the table. Matilda, set the cups and plates out. Sarah, you'll be in charge of cleaning the dishes after dinner."

The boy cupped Celeste in his hands. "That's her, that's Mama. Supper's on the table. You just be still and stay outta Pa's way."

"John, wash those hands! They're filthy!" Mama called out, louder. "Abe!"

Celeste felt a jerk as the boy sat up and climbed down the loft ladder. "Yes, ma'am!" he called out.

"Abe," Celeste said to herself. "That's the boy's name."

Still in the pocket of her new human friend, Celeste cautiously peeked out. The family had gathered around the rustic table, three girls and a boy squeezed together, and Mama at one end. A gruff-looking man sat opposite. Mama glanced at him.

"Pa, will you say grace?"

The family bowed their heads, and the man spoke.

"Oh Lord, for this food we are about to receive, make us truly grateful. Amen."

Celeste saw everyone gaze with hungry anticipation at the meager meal: a lean chicken, roasted over the fireplace, a steaming bowl of boiled pumpkin, biscuits, and a pitcher of frothy milk.

"Get the firewood like I told you?" Pa asked gruffly.

Abe looked up as he pulled at a chicken wing. "Yes, sir," he answered.

"Abe added plenty to the pile out front, and filled the wood box up, too," Mama added. "Fine job." She turned to the boy and smiled. "You put in a full day of chores today, son."

"Abe's arms and legs are growing faster than the rest of him," said one of the girls, laughing. "I'll wager he can outrun a bear!"

Abe grinned back. "And I'll wager you'd be right, Sarah. Let's have a bear race after dinner. You go find the bear."

Everyone laughed at the thought of a bear and the lanky boy in a footrace. All except Pa, who stood and scowled at Abe.

"Tomorrow, make sure the rest of the corn is all husked and stored away. No dawdlin'."

"Yes, sir."

Abe secretly took a piece of his biscuit and plopped it down into his vest pocket. Celeste sniffed, then took a nibble. It was soft and slightly doughy. She peeked out the buttonhole of the pocket.

She watched cautiously as the family ate their dinner. The other boy at the end of the table took a gulp of milk. "I saw a big flock of turkeys today, down by the creek," he said. He wiped his mouth with the back of his hand. "Big flock. Lost count at a hun'erd."

"If you saw a hun'erd turkeys, how come there ain't no turkey meat on the table tonight?" Pa asked, scowling at the young boy.

The boy looked down at his plate, deflated. "Didn't have my rifle," he replied.

"Hmph."

Mama glanced at Abe hopefully. Abe chuckled. "You lost count, John, because you started thinking about roast turkey!"

The other children giggled, and John smiled.

Abe continued, "John, did I ever tell you about the time I saw a turkey peckin' at gunpowder?"

Matilda and Elizabeth's eye widened, and John grinned. "Gunpowder? Why would a turkey eat gunpowder?"

"Don't know, but this one did," Abe continued. "Guess he was mighty hungry. And he ate so much gunpowder he could barely stand on his own two legs. Heavy as a big bag of lead shot!"

The children giggled some more. Celeste saw their faces, glowing in the light from the fireplace, as they hung on Abe's every word.

"What happened next?" Elizabeth asked.

"Well, seems this ol' turkey was so heavy with gunpowder, and so wobbly on his legs, he had to sit down. An' he sat right down on a lit match!"

The children and Mama burst into laughter at

the thought, and even Pa grinned.

"And then what?" Matilda begged.

"Well, let's jus' say that Thanksgiving came early that year. Wasn't much left to slice up, but we had mighty tasty turkey fritters. An' it just goes to say, always look before you sit!"

The children broke into peals of laughter as the mood at the table changed from tense to merry, and Mama gave Abe a grateful smile.

"You can tell a good story," Pa said. "That I'll give you."

"Tell another one, Abe," Sarah insisted. But dinner was over, and dishes had to be done, and chores finished for the day. Abe, with Celeste still in his pocket, headed out to the cowshed to give Bet and Bright some hay.

Abe paused to take in the beauty of the night. The stars were out, the night clear as well water.

He looked down at Celeste staring up from his vest pocket. "You don't mind ridin' around in there, do you?" He grinned. "Just keep out of Pa's way, and you'll be fine."

CHAPTER FIFTEEN
Frontier Life

Then came days that Celeste passed by exploring the cabin . . . carefully, so as not to catch the attention of Abe's father . . . and becoming acquainted with Abe. It took a while to get used to Abe's walking pace; his long, lanky legs made for long strides, so different from Joseph's quick movements.

Abe was different from Joseph in other ways, too. Where Joseph would stroke and caress Celeste, and use her as a model for his sketches, Abe seemed to forget she was even there. He would look to be totally absorbed in thought, then suddenly glance down at his vest pocket, and as if noticing Celeste for the first time, would say, "Hello, friend!" and then go about his chores.

Even though food in the house wasn't plentiful, Abe provided tidbits for his little mouse. He made a spot for her to sleep next to his pallet, a little wooden box that had lost its lid, with a flannel rag tucked inside.

After a time, Abe got more and more used to having a mouse accompanying him everywhere, and more and more attentive. He started saving bits of crusts and other scraps for Celeste.

One late afternoon, Celeste was in Abe's shirt pocket. Suddenly, the boy sat upright and then peeked through the deerskin window. "Turkey!" he whispered. "Right out in front of the house. A whole flock."

He grabbed the shotgun that always was ready and at hand, leaning by the door. He poked the barrel of the gun carefully through a crack in the wall, and aimed.

Blast! A roar ripped through the cold afternoon air as the shotgun kicked back. Immediately, the smell of gunpowder smoke filled the little room. They heard the turkeys scramble through the underbrush.

Abe walked outside and then stood over a turkey that didn't escape the gunshot pellets. He picked up the turkey by its feet; its wings fell limply, splayed and lifeless.

Celeste squirmed in Abe's pocket. The blast of the shotgun had nearly deafened her. And the limp turkey's blank eyes made her shiver. She looked up at Abe.

His face had turned pale and sad. "I'll never kill again," he said.

The days were cold now, and short. Whenever anyone came through the cabin door, a gust of cold wind came in, too. The nights were long and very dark. Mama would brighten the little cabin by burning pine knots, or a little bowl of bear grease. The only heat came from the fireplace, and the family huddled around it every night.

Abe would gently scoop Celeste up each time he went for one of his many chores.

He was in charge of feeding the small chicken flock, and tending to Bet and Bright. The cows had to be fed and watered, and milked twice a day, morning and evening.

And, of course, there was chopping wood. Firewood was a vital necessity for cooking the meals and for heating the cabin. Keeping the hearth stacked with firewood was an endless chore, and Abe's skills at swinging an ax became as honed as the blade itself.

All the children collected nuts and berries when they were in season. Celeste took long rides in Abe's coat pocket, or rode upon the brim of his hat as he gathered baskets of chestnuts and walnuts and hickory nuts, or bags of persimmons or crab apples or wild plums.

Water had to be carried daily from the creek. It was a long walk to the nearest source of fresh water, and it seemed like Abe was always plodding down the familiar path to the creek, wooden bucket in each hand. Abe would stuff a corn dodger or two into the pockets of his pants as he did his chores, giving Celeste bits and pieces during the day.

Celeste thought of Hazel and Chester and the rest of her friends out in the woods, and wondered how they were faring. She pictured her little nook, with its tiny supply of food that she had gathered, and shuddered when she realized that it wouldn't have been nearly enough to last these many weeks.

Then the snow came.

The first storm of the winter slid over the landscape, approaching from the south, cold and heavy. The sullen, gray sky made it feel like evening all day long. Celeste poked her head beneath the door just as white flakes began to fall. She watched them, uneasy but entranced. As the storm descended in earnest, the flakes covered the ground quickly; Celeste didn't know it would be the last time she'd see brown earth until spring.

The two sturdy horses, Bet and Bright, stood with their backs to the wind. Other than an occasional shake of their manes, the only sound was that of the snow falling. Celeste listened and heard the tiny flakes

land on one another like jasmine blossoms on cotton balls, barely audible puffs of winter.

And snow had a new smell, clean and fresh, so different from the tea-colored bayous and musky

hanging moss of Oakley.

By the end of the day, the ground was masked by a white blanket, the landscape changed. The snow towered over her.

One morning, Abe slipped Celeste into his coat pocket and headed out across the snowy landscape. He traipsed over a mile through the woods, up steep embankments and down along narrow hollows, until at last they came to a small settlement. A few drab dwellings and other small buildings were dotted around. "Pigeon Creek," Abe said. "It ain't much."

He walked hesitantly up to a wood-clad cabin. "Here we are. Schoolhouse."

He stepped inside. A small coal stove was trying in vain to heat even one side of the narrow room. A slate chalkboard hung on one wall, but there was very little else to denote it was a schoolroom.

Several boys and girls were sitting on wooden benches, and stared at Abe as he entered.

Abe took off his hat and quietly took a seat on one of the benches.

A man standing at the front of the room greeted him. He was tall, with a tangle of red hair, and wore a black woolen coat. "Ah! Abe. Good to see you again."

Celeste could see the man's breath in the air, even though they were inside.

"Thank you, Mr. Swaney," Abe said.

"It's been several months."

"Yes, sir."

"Not easy keeping up with chores spring, summer, and fall, and coming to school, isn't that so?"

"Yes, sir. Mama sent me here this mornin'."

"Have you been keeping up with learning your alphabet?"

Abe looked around, fiddling with the brim of his hat. "I reckon not as good as I could be," he replied.

Mr. Swaney smiled. "Well, we'll bring you up to snuff.

We're working on that right now."

The children followed along with Mr. Swaney as he scribbled different shapes on the slate board, or used a wooden pointer to pick out certain letters or words to recite. Celeste watched, still hidden away in Abe's pocket.

At midday, Abe pulled a corn dodger from a pocket, sharing a bit of it with Celeste. After an afternoon of counting and adding numbers, Abe headed back into the cold. "Long walk for a day of schoolin'," Abe said to himself as he trudged along. "And not many days of it, when you put them all together. But I'll learn to read and write yet."

The sun was very low. It was dark by the time he got home.

CHAPTER SIXTEEN
Learning to Read

The long distance and the cold winter made more treks to Pigeon Creek difficult and sporadic. Abe was limited to practicing his reading at home. In the evening, the family gathered around the smoky fireplace, or crawled under their quilts to stay warm. Pa would whittle or smoke his pipe quietly. Mama would knit or patch torn clothing with needle and thread. Celeste would curl up, warm and snug in Abe's pocket, listening to the pops and crackles of the hickory logs burning.

Abe would stare into the flames, thinking. Sometimes he would pull down one of the few books that sat perched on a shelf, and then trace along with his finger, rough and callused, the magical shapes and figures that marched in rows across each page.

Celeste would poke her pink nose and dark eyes over the edge of the vest pocket and follow along, too.

At first, the little symbols on the pages looked like fleas on a white dog to Celeste . . . and it seemed as though Abe thought the same thing. He struggled slowly over each letter. Finishing each sentence was harder than hauling water uphill.

Mama would glance up from her needlework and see him getting frustrated.

"The more you learn, the more you'll be able to help others," she would say.

"Yes, Mama."

"And the better you are at reading, the more you'll learn. Now start again and read me another sentence."

After weeks and weeks of watching and listening, Celeste began to see something: Abe understood that certain symbols meant certain sounds. The sounds put together meant human words.

Word by word and page by page, Abe became more confident.

The day was cold, clear, and windless. The bare oaks and chestnuts glistened against the glare of the blue-white snow. Abe, with Celeste snug in his wool coat pocket, was out in the small barn, tending to the cows. Belle was giving him a half pailful of frothy, warm milk. "Good girl," he said. "Mama will make some biscuits with this, I reckon." He gave the brown cow a pat. She eyed him patiently, her breath coming out in steamy clouds.

Outside, Pa was perched on top of the smokehouse, braving the cold and repairing the roof. "Half a pail, Pa," Abe hollered up. "I hope ol' Belle don't go dry," he added. Pa nodded.

Back inside the little cabin, Abe draped his coat over a chair near the fireplace, and then poured the milk into an earthenware crock. Mama was busy stirring something over the fire; she didn't notice Celeste as she wiggled out from the vest pocket and made her way along the top of the dresser.

The shelves above were lined with an assortment of interesting things: crocks, a pitcher, a jar of feathers used to make quill pens, and several books.

Celeste sniffed at the books. They smelled of leather, and also of a musty, inky paper. She studied the brown leather spines. They had markings that reminded her

of the shapes that Abe scrawled on the slate at school.

"Stew's on," Mama said absently. She cut chunks of warm corn bread from an iron skillet. "Wash up, before it gets cold."

"Thanks, Mama," Abe answered. He hurriedly washed his hands in a crock full of melted snow. He noticed a shadow move across the shelf in front of him, and looked up to see Celeste nosing her way across the books.

"What are you doing?" he whispered. "You're not supposed to be wanderin' around!" He gathered Celeste up in his hand, putting her in his vest pocket. He glanced back at a book on the shelf. "*F . . . F . . .*" he stuttered, studying the book's spine. He thought for a moment, and then slid the book off the shelf.

"What's Abe doin', lookin' at a book for?" Matilda asked.

"He's gonna eat it for dinner." John giggled.

"Abe! Food is on the table!" Pa hollered.

Abe tucked the book next to him on the wooden bench. The corn bread was buttery. The stew was thick, with potatoes and corn and venison. Abe savored every bite, glancing repeatedly at the book by his side. "*F . . . A*," he whispered to himself.

The dishes were cleaned and put away. Another log was thrown onto the fire, and Abe sat in its orange glow, studying the book in front of him. Celeste perched on the edge of the book.

"*F*," he said quietly. "*F. FA*." He glanced up at Celeste, who swished her tail this way and that, straight, curved, following along and making the letters as Abe said them. Abe grinned. "Yes, that's right," he said. "*F* and *A*."

He kept at it, repeating the letters as Celeste formed them. "*F . . . A . . . B . . . L . . . E . . . S . . .*" he read, following along with his finger and touching each letter. "*F . . . A*. I got it! *Fables!*"

Celeste flicked her tail this way and that in

congratulations. Abe continued his attempts, with Celeste helping along. "Fables," he said proudly. "Next. *O. F.* That spells *of.* Now *A . . . E . . . S . . . O . . . P. Aesop. Fables of Aesop!*" Celeste wiggled her tail, forming the letters in rapid succession, Abe laughing out loud with delight.

Mama looked over the quilt she was stitching, puzzled. "What have you got there?" she asked.

"Nothin', Mama. Just learnin' my letters." He quickly slipped Celeste into his pocket.

Eventually, the family went to bed, all except Abe.

The fire crackled and sizzled. Outside, under a half-moon, a great gray owl called out through the trees and across the frozen, crusty snow. Another owl answered back. Abe continued to struggle across the page, with Celeste quietly acting as his assistant. The letters came a little easier as they kept going. As the fire dimmed and bedtime drew near, Abe was several sentences into page one.

One evening, Mama looked up at Abe, who was laboring over one of *Fables of Aesop*. She rummaged through her sewing basket and found a pencil stub. "Sharpen this for me, Pa," she said.

Pa whittled the tip of the stubby pencil.

She gave it to Abe. "You should be learning your letters. Writin' is just as important as readin'."

"What do I practice on?"

Mama hesitated, glancing around the room. Paper was a rare commodity. "You can practice on the back of that wooden spoon."

Abe planted himself in front of the fire with the large wooden mixing spoon in his lap. Celeste watched as he took the pencil stub and began writing across the flat bowl of the spoon, slowly and methodically, almost painfully.

"Start yourself out simple," Mama instructed. "Just the first ten letters. But I want 'em wrote out ten times. Ten."

Celeste watched from the vest pocket, fascinated with the curves and bends and tiny lines of the letters. She watched closely as Abe laboriously drew the shapes in a row across the wooden spoon. Once he'd run out of room, he'd rub his letters out and start again. But he grew frustrated.

"Mama, I don't think I can do any more tonight."

Mama looked at him patiently. Scrawling the

letters seemed to mean something important to her. "All right," she said. "But I've got it in my mind that you're going to be the one in the family to read *and* to write. And make something of yourself! Now head up to bed."

Each night was much the same, as Abe struggled with his reading and writing in front of the fire. He would get frustrated and want to give up; reading the letters felt like getting corn to grow in a drought. But between his stepmother's prodding and Celeste's dark brown eyes encouraging him, he kept at it.

One night, Celeste peeked down from the loft. The living room was quiet, the fireplace just glowing embers, although the wind roared through the treetops outside. She crept down the ladder, scurried to the sewing basket, and crawled inside. She found the pencil, and then carefully carried it back up the wooden pegs to Abe's sleeping loft. There, she sat for a while and chewed the stubby point until it was sharp again, then laid it next to Abe's pillow. "Maybe that will help him practice," she said to herself, curling once again into a ball in her sleeping box.

When Abe awoke just before daylight, he found himself staring at the sharpened pencil. "Now, how do you suppose . . . ?" he murmured.

Celeste watched, whiskers twitching.

The next evening, Abe sat before a smooth shake

shingle and tried again. This time Celeste sat on the edge of the shingle and watched his every line, every stroke. She tried to copy the letters, using her tail to mimic the shape. When he made a straight line, her tail was straight; when he curved a line for a letter, Celeste's tail arced and curled. The more Abe practiced, the more Celeste did, too.

Abe watched, half-amused, half-amazed, as Celeste's tail flicked this way and that. As he wrote a *C*, Celeste's tail became a *C*. He wrote an *D*, and Celeste's tail was straight, and then a curved arc.

"All right . . . something tough!" he said, and drew a *K*.

Celeste's tail stuck straight up, then at an angle up, then at an angle down.

Abe's eyes lit up. "Let's do some more."

They practiced and practiced as the fire turned to embers, and then to ashes. Then Abe lit a precious candle, and they practiced some more.

CHAPTER SEVENTEEN

A New Book for Abe

The winter seemed to stall, and the days trick-led by like the water in the creek, cold, barely moving, and under a blanket of snow. Abe spent them doing chores, tending to the animals, or clean-ing game that Pa brought home. Evenings were spent in front of the fire, reading *Fables of Aesop*, letter by letter, sentence by sentence. It took a while, but eventually Abe and Celeste came to the end. It only made Abe want to start another one.

Celeste scampered across the top of the desk, sniffing at the books. "*The Pilgrim's Progress*," Abe recited as Celeste sniffed at the spine. "That sounds interesting. We're making progress, too, mouse!" They sat in front of the fire and began again.

Now the words seemed to flow across the page; instead of being roadblocks, they became roads, and around every bend was a new adventure. The winter was not over, and Abe had exhausted the tiny library in the cabin.

But one evening as a snowstorm swept across the countryside, a neighbor came by the cabin. Josiah Crawford was caught out in the weather, too far to travel home.

"Stay here tonight, Josiah," Pa said. "No sense in trying to head over yonder to your place. We'll make room."

Mama looked drawn but cut up another potato and added it to the rabbit stew that bubbled in a pot over the fire. "Sit yourself down," she said. "Shake the cold off."

After a dinner of stew, they sat in front of the fire, and Abe took his place at the hearth, book in hand. He had almost finished *Progress*.

Mr. Crawford watched the boy as he read. His eyebrows arched in surprise. "How'd you learn to read so good, boy?" he asked. "You're makin' good time!"

"Thank you, sir," Abe replied. "I been practicin'. Night after night, all winter. Gettin' pretty good."

"You might be interested in a book or two of mine. You're welcome to borrow them. If you want, you can come fetch them anytime."

Abe gave Mr. Crawford a broad smile. "I'd be much obliged," he said.

The man lit his pipe. "Anytime," he replied.

As soon after the storm as he could, Abe tucked Celeste into his coat pocket and headed out. The air was brittle and frozen. A fresh snow disguised the woods and fields, adding another smooth layer of white. It hid the features of the landscape and was disorienting.

Celeste poked her head out of Abe's coat pocket and looked in wonder at the startling landscape. The snow was piled high in mounds, like cotton bolls, on every surface. It reminded her of the cotton wagon, long ago in the summer, and of that fateful day she rode it to the river wharf. Her heart gave a little twisty leap as she thought of Joseph, and her life in another place. She looked up at Abe, who gave her a smile and stroked her ears. "Hey, mouse," he said comfortingly. She burrowed down into the warmth of his pocket.

"Hello, boy!" Mr. Crawford called out as he saw Abe trudging through the drifts. "Come to get your book?"

"Yes, sir," Abe answered, his voice muffled by the white masses of powdery snow. The Crawfords' cabin was a bit more luxurious than Abe's. It was larger, with a big brick chimney and fireplace. Over the fireplace hung a gilded mirror, and there was more furniture dotted through the two rooms.

Mr. Crawford led Abe to a shelf that hung over a writing desk. "Take your pick," he said proudly, pointing to a double row of books. "Any one but that one." He pulled a thick, black leather book out, tattered and well thumbed. "Family Bible," he noted. "That one stays here. Any of the others you're welcome to borrow."

Abe eyed them with amazement. They were all so tempting. Selecting any one of them meant spending the remaining winter evenings in another world, learning new things. He ran his finger along the spines of the red, brown, and black leather bindings. Finally, his fingers lingered on *The Life and Memorable Actions of George Washington*, and he pulled it out. "This one, Mr. Crawford?" he asked.

"Sure enough! Good choice, son. You're going to like that one. Just make sure you bring it back in one piece."

"Yes, sir! I'll bring it back just like you see it now," Abe said. "Thank you, sir. I'm much obliged."

"Not at all, not at all. You're going to make yourself into a well-read young man, Abe. Next thing you
know, you'll have folks from hither and yonder askin'
you your thoughts on the world. Mark my words!"

Abe grinned as he waved good-bye to Mr.
Crawford, and he and Celeste plunged back into

the knee-high snow, mak-
ing their way home across
the fields and through the
woods.

Nearer to home, they
came to what seemed like
a familiar area. Celeste
recognized the slope of
the land and the size and
shape of the trees. She
looked up to see a giant
white pine and a collec-
tion of sticks and leaves

tucked into a crotch of branches; it looked like a nest she had seen before . . . Chester and Hazel's nest! She chattered and squeaked with excitement, trying to call out to the two squirrels, but they were much too high above the snowdrifts.

"What in tarnation is the matter with you?" Abe laughed. "You're upset about something!"

Celeste gazed after the giant pine as they moved away through the snow and the tree got farther and farther away. She remembered the day months ago when she was rescued by the two friendly squirrels and the little family of woodland mice that looked after her.

I wonder how they're all doing, she thought to herself. *Hazel, and Chester, Monroe, and Pawpaw?* She looked down, from the edge of Abe's pocket, to the ground. The snow was cold and deep. She remembered how the winter had been filled with howling winds that roared through the bare tree limbs, and the way the

sleet had hammered at the shingled roof like a million tiny woodpeckers. She shivered as she thought of her friends, somehow bundled up against the cold, hopefully keeping dry and warm.

The sun was nearly disappearing below the crest of a southwestern hill when they arrived back at the little cabin. Abe tracked in little piles of snow as he

stomped his feet and shook off his coat. Mama had made a pot of sassafras tea. The aroma filled the room.

He settled down in front of the fire, with Celeste curled in the crook of his elbow. He turned to page one of *George Washington*.

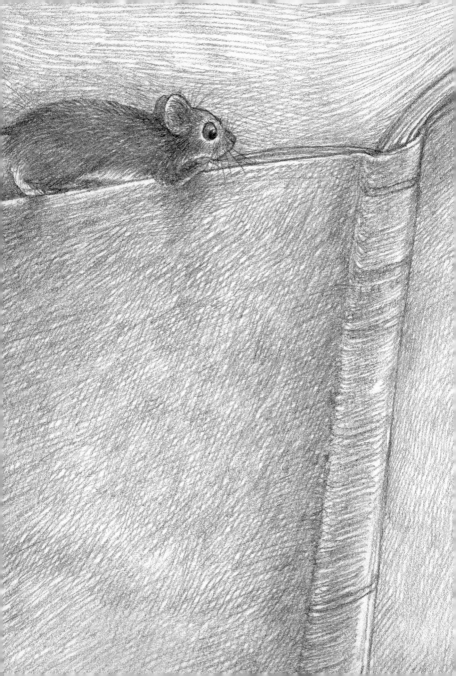

CHAPTER EIGHTEEN
Water-Soaked

It was a struggle, but Abe and Celeste began George's long journey, chapter by chapter. As Abe read, slowly at first, then more quickly, Celeste followed along. One letter after another, one word leading to another, she encouraged Abe with her bright brown eyes. She would scamper across the page, leading

Abe onward. Every night, Abe would tuck the book into a special niche in the wall next to his corn-husk mattress, between two chestnut logs where the mud chinking had loosened and fallen out.

At last, April arrived, and March released its frosty grip on the landscape. The cold, stiff winds of winter were gone, replaced with blustery spring showers.

A front moved through, bringing a chilly, drenching rain that soaked the thawing ground. Abe was chopping wood, his coat and hat doing their best to keep him dry. Celeste was curled up in her wooden box, asleep.

Suddenly, a dousing drop of cold rain hit her head. She woke with a start, then looked up: another leak in the roof. There had been many over the winter. As she tucked herself into a drier corner of the box, she saw the copy of *George Washington*.

The sheets of blowing rain outside had run down

the chestnut logs, and into the spot where the book was sitting. It was unprotected, and the book was getting soaked. Celeste sprang out of the box and looked around; an old handkerchief lay nearby. She quickly grabbed the corner of it between her teeth and dragged it over to the book. With several maneuvers, she was able to pull and yank the handkerchief over the book, protecting it a little.

Her heart raced as she examined the book. It was squishy, the pages completely water-soaked. The leather cover and binding were ruined. *Abe won't like this, not one bit*, she thought to herself. *And he promised Mr. Crawford he'd return it in one piece.* She climbed on top of the book. Trying to lift the pages only caused them to tear.

She waited all afternoon and into the evening for Abe to finish his chores. Finally, as the light was fading, he returned. He climbed up the peg ladder to the sleeping loft, and gave Celeste a few strokes behind the ear, as well as a walnut meat. "Hey, little mouse," he said with a tired voice. She looked at him with worried eyes as he reached for the sodden book, and then she saw the color drain from his face. His jaw dropped.

"Oh . . . oh," Abe whispered. "I've ruined Mr. Crawford's book! He'll never let me borrow another one. How am I ever gonna repay him?"

Celeste watched as he collapsed, his face in the blanket.

CHAPTER NINETEEN
Reunion

Celeste rode on top of Abe's worn hat as he trudged dejectedly across the woods and fields to the Crawfords' place. Even though the day was a pleasant one, Abe's mood was sour and angry. Replacing Mr. Crawford's book would take a long time; books were extravagant luxuries, and very expensive. Paying off the debt would certainly mean chores, and lots of them.

Celeste watched the countryside go by as she bobbed up and down with Abe's long strides. The last bits of persistent snow, clutching in patches to north-facing slopes, had disappeared. The hills were now soft and damp; the sun was pulling the sweet moisture from the ground. Trees were coming back to life. The ends of each branch and twig were painted with pale green as their buds popped open. Birds sang among the buds.

As Abe walked near a dogwood tree, a pair of pewees began calling to each other from overhead. Abe stopped, and the pewees began swooping from branch to branch, frantically calling out. "Go away! Don't come any nearer!"

Celeste stood on the brim of the hat and yelled up to them. "What's the matter?" she squeaked. "What's wrong?"

But before the pewees could answer, Abe had removed his hat, with Celeste still perched on it, and placed it carefully on the ground. He put the damaged book next to the hat.

Then he bent down and, very gently, scooped up something in his hands.

The distraught pewees stopped their frenzied cries for a moment and stared, disbelieving, as Abe located a nest in the dogwood branches overhead. Then he carefully placed a baby pewee back in its home, next to its sibling.

"There ya go," Abe said.

The adult pewees, fluttering and chirping in relief, returned to their babies. "Thank you!" one of them hollered down. "I didn't know humans could be like that!"

"You're welcome," Celeste squeaked back up. "And yes! This human is the kind that likes to help the helpless!"

Abe, amused at the all the chirping and squeaking going on all around him, picked up his hat and, with Celeste still hanging on, placed it back on his head. He tucked the copy of *George Washington* inside his shirt, and then started again toward the Crawford place.

Along the way, they passed the low wetland. Forest and Chloe were busy at work. From her high perch, Celeste could see two Vs moving across the water surface as the beavers busily went about their business.

"Hello!" she squeaked. Forest stopped in the water and, mouth full of willow branches, slapped a hello with his tail.

After a while, Abe and Celeste arrived at the Crawford cabin. Abe suddenly was looking all the more dejected as he slipped Celeste into his shirt pocket.

"Well, here goes nothin'," he said to himself. "I hope Mr. Crawford ain't too hard on me."

Mrs. Crawford came to the door, wiping her hands on her apron. "Abe!" she said cheerily. "Nice to see you. What brings you 'round this way?"

Abe nervously cleared his throat.

"Miz Crawford, ma'am? Is Mr. Crawford home?"

"He's over at the Grigsbys' place. What's your business with Mr. Crawford, Abe?"

Celeste looked up out of the pocket and saw Abe looking miserable as he took a deep breath. "I've done ruined Mr. Crawford's fine book, ma'am." He pulled the sodden book out from within his shirt and held it up. "It got soaked in the rain. It ain't worth nothin' now."

Mrs. Crawford squinted at the book, frowning. Books were precious and expensive. But she saw Abe's distraught face. "Well, now, Abe. Don't go worryin' yourself into a crazy person. It ain't the end of the world."

"Mr. Crawford may think different," Abe replied as he watched Mrs. Crawford try to open the soggy pages. "I don't want him to have feelin's against me."

"Mr. Crawford would never have ill feelings for

you, Abe. He was just telling me the other day how much he enjoyed your storytelling and your way with words."

"I don't aim to lose Mr. Crawford as a friend. My best friend is the man who'll loan me a book I ain't read yet."

Mrs. Crawford smiled. "What do you have in mind, Abe?"

"You got any chores you need doin'?" Abe asked hopefully. "I aim to repay Mr. Crawford by maybe helpin' with his chores."

"Now, Abe, you have your own chores to do. Your ma may not like you spending your chore time here!"

Abe frowned. "I ain't got any money, Miz Crawford. Doin' chores is the only thing I can do to repay him."

Just then, a blue jay landed on the woodpile nearby. Mrs. Crawford thought a moment. "You want to chop us some wood? I hear you've got a talent for that. We

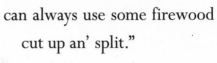

can always use some firewood cut up an' split."

"Yes, ma'am! I can cut wood for you. Tomorrow's Sunday. I can start day after."

"That'll be fine, Abe. I'll tell Mr. Crawford."

Abe put his hat back on. "Thank you, ma'am," he said, setting off into the woods. He put Celeste back on his hat. "Lots of work to do, mouse," he said quietly. "I'll be choppin' wood the rest of my life."

Celeste smiled as they set off again, with Celeste still perched on the brim of Abe's hat. They passed beneath a giant white pine, and Celeste suddenly

sat upright. Scampering
across the huge trunk
of the pine were Hazel
and Chester, chas-
ing each other in
corkscrew patterns
around and around.

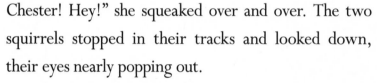

Celeste was nearly
giddy with joy. "Hazel!
Chester! Hey!" she squeaked over and over. The two
squirrels stopped in their tracks and looked down,
their eyes nearly popping out.

"Celeste?" they shouted in unison. "Celeste!"

"Yes!" she called back. "I'm so happy to see you!"

Abe stopped in his tracks, too, and carefully took
his hat off. He gave Celeste a curious look. "What
th' heck's the matter, mouse?"
he asked.

Hazel and Chester were still chattering and flicking their tails like pompoms. Abe looked at them, and then back again at Celeste. "You're talkin' squirrel talk!" he said with awe. He placed his hat on the ground.

Celeste scampered off and quickly made her way through the leaf litter to the base of the white pine. "Hello!" she said again as Hazel and Chester clambered down the tree to greet her. They raced in circles around Celeste, who raced in circles around them, all three of them chittering and laughing. Abe stood silent, watching in wonder. "What . . . ?" he murmured to himself.

Celeste and the two squirrels all spoke at once.

"Where have you *been*?"

"What *happened* to you?"

"We thought for sure the winter had gotten you!"

"How is Pawpaw? And Monroe? And Forest, and Chloe?"

"Why are you with the *human*?"

Celeste tried to catch them up on everything that had happened during the long, cold winter. Hazel's whiskers twitched with amazement when Celeste told them about the cabin, the warm fire, and the human named Abe, who fed her bits of food, and with whom she explored books all winter long. The three friends glanced over at the boy, who was still standing some distance away, staring in disbelief.

"He looks silly." Hazel giggled.

"I'd better get back to him," Celeste said.

"Huh?" Chester squeaked. "Back?"

"Yes. He has to replace a . . . well, I have to help him, that's all."

"Huh?" the two squirrels said at once.

Celeste thought a moment more. "Where is Forest?" she asked.

"Oh, around here somewhere," Chester replied.

"Get him to come to the cabin in the hollow

tonight. Midnight. You two come, too. And tell Pawpaw and Monroe, too, if you see them. Tell them it's important."

"Why? What are you planning?"

"I'm getting an idea. Forest can help, I'm sure of it. You can, too."

CHAPTER TWENTY
Celeste's Plan

Celeste had a plan. If she could talk her friends into helping, they might be able to make short work of Abe's wood-chopping task . . . at least a little.

She looked out between the chinks in the log walls. It was nearly midnight. Off in the distance, she could hear the soft rustling of feet coming through the dry leaves of the woods floor. In a moment, she saw the dark shapes of Forest and Chloe, lumbering across the ground. Immediately after them scampered Hazel and Chester, and Pawpaw and Monroe. In a flash, Celeste scurried between the logs and out into the damp night.

"Thanks for coming, everyone," she whispered to the little group. "We have a lot to do tonight."

"What are we doing here, Celeste?" Forest asked, looking a bit grumpy.

"We're here to help Abe out," Celeste replied. "He has to cut wood for the man in the next holler. Forest, you and Chloe are the best woodcutters I know. Can you cut down a tree tonight?"

The two beavers looked at each other and grinned. "Watch us," Chloe said. "Where's the tree and where do you want it to land?"

"I knew I could count on you," replied Celeste. "We'll need to get near this other man's cabin. We'll locate a tree that will do, and then you can go to work." She turned to the two squirrels. "You two can chew off the smaller branches. We'll make short work of it."

"What can we do?" asked Pawpaw.

Celeste smiled, her whiskers twitching. "I need you for moral support. Also, for helping with giving directions."

The two mice flicked their tails. "We can do that!" Monroe said proudly.

They set off into the woods, winding their way through the thick vegetation before finally getting near the Crawford cabin.

Celeste leaped onto a rock. "All right," she directed. "Forest, you're good at choosing trees. Can you pick us out a good one?"

"Easy as chewing through a willow twig," he said confidently. He surveyed the surrounding trees, and in no time had selected a medium-sized oak, and figured where and how it would fall.

"Perfect," Celeste said. "Cut 'er down!"

Forest and Chloe got to work immediately, chewing in circles at the base of tree, around and around, never seeming to tire, until at last the oak began to teeter.

"Here she comes!" shouted Forest, and the oak leaned farther to one side, then came swooshing down through the leafy understory, landing on the ground with a crash.

"Nice job," cheered Celeste. "Now let's get to work, everybody."

Hazel and Chester began at one end of the oak, and Chloe and Forest at the other, nibbling and chewing off the twigs and smaller branches and

dragging them away from the fallen trunk. They
worked together as a team, efficiently disman-
tling the tree until it was daybreak.

They followed much the same routine

the next night, with Chloe and Forest chewing the trunk and limbs. By Monday morning, they had stripped the tree. It was perfectly prepared for an ax to reduce it to firewood.

Abe's ax.

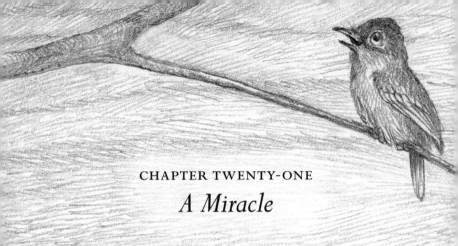

CHAPTER TWENTY-ONE
A Miracle

Early Monday morning, Abe, with Celeste perched on his hat, picked up his ax and headed across the fields and woods toward the Crawford homestead. Abe whistled a tune as he loped along, and Celeste bobbed and swayed with his long strides, enjoying the view.

He was barefoot. His worn leather shoes had lasted through the winter; he wouldn't be putting shoes on again until autumn, after the first frost.

Birds were singing brightly and the air was coming alive with springtime. They passed patches of bloodwort and spring beauties popping up from the leaf litter in the woods. Buttercups had braved the chill morning and now basked in the warm sunshine. Lavender-pink redbud and creamy white dogwood blossoms dotted the understory.

After they crossed the small creek and headed up the slope to the Crawfords' cabin, Abe stopped in his tracks. A large oak tree lay prostrate and stripped of its branches in front of him.

"What . . . ? Well, I'll be!" he murmured to himself. "What goes on here?" He hurried up the hill to the cabin.

Mr. Crawford was in the little chicken coop, tending to the small flock. "No, don't know about any trees down," he said. "But I appreciate the way you want to replace the book, Abe. You're an honest boy."

Abe hurried back to the downed tree and quickly surveyed the scene. He took his ax in hand and began the process of turning the oak into fireplace-sized

logs. As it was already down, the work was cut in half, literally.

With strong, even whacks, Abe cut each limb into short lengths. The thick pieces of the trunk were split into smaller chunks. By the end of the day, he had tackled and completed half the work. Celeste sat on his hat in the shade, watching his progress with interest.

Most of the next day was spent finishing the splitting, and then hauling the firewood, one heavy armful at a time, from the sunny hillside to the Crawford cabin, and stacking it piece by piece. The dense chunks of wood were placed carefully one on top of another, like pieces of a puzzle, so that they fit efficiently, and the stack wouldn't topple.

By the end of the third day, his work was done, the book "paid" for.

"Don't know how this tree ended up here, just

sittin' waitin' for me, but I'm mighty
grateful to . . . to whoever!" Abe
said to himself, his black hair
sticking to his damp fore-
head, and his eyes
still looking

a bit amazed at his good luck. His homespun shirt was dark with sweat after the day of cutting and splitting and stacking the wood.

The book had been repaid. A large supply of firewood sat neatly stacked near the Crawfords' cabin door.

Celeste thought of Forest and Chloe, who had done much of the work, and Hazel and Chester, who had energetically rallied and tackled the smaller pieces. She smiled to herself.

With Abe's help, Celeste had made it through the winter. Now spring was in full bloom, with summer on its way. The tall trees rustled their new, mint-green leaves. Birdsong echoed throughout the woods.

Celeste sat atop Abe's gray hat, as they walked through the woods. Abe was quiet and pensive.

"Mouse," he said quietly, almost to himself, "I

think there's a whole library over in Boonville, full of books. All kinds of books. It's only about sixteen miles. We should go sometime. I aim to read 'em all."

Celeste's whiskers flickered with satisfaction.

They headed home.

CHAPTER TWENTY-TWO
Celeste's Choice

A be!"

Pa's voice came rumbling across the muddy yard of the homestead.

Celeste climbed out of her wooden box and peered through a crack between the chinked logs. The morning sun was just peeking through the chestnut leaves. Abe was racing to the shed.

"Make sure you get the harness oiled before tomorrow."

"Yes, Pa."

"We gotta get over to Hatfield in the morning, then over t' the river. Boat's comin' in. We'll get some supplies from down south."

Celeste gave a little start. River? *Boat?*

She scampered down the chinked logs of the cabin, and cautiously but quickly made her way past the edge of the horse pasture, hoping to find Hazel or Chester nearby. Sure enough, she heard them chittering up the wooded hillside on a hickory limb.

"Hello!" Chester called out when he saw Celeste darting between the vines and wildflowers on the forest floor. "What brings you out on this fine morning?"

"Good morning, Chester. Good morning, Hazel. I just heard something very exciting!"

Hazel flicked her bushy tail. "What's up, honey?"

"Abe is heading to the river tomorrow. The river!"

"Is that so?" Hazel replied.

"What's so very excitin' about that?" Chester asked.

"Well, it means that Abe and Pa are going to be

near a boat. Maybe a steamboat! A boat that heads south, down the river!"

Chester frowned. "Hmm. And you want to hitch a ride on a steamboat, same's you did gettin' here?"

"Yes!"

Hazel's tail drooped. "You sure you want to leave us, Celeste? I don't mind tellin' you, I'd be near brokenhearted."

"I'm feelin' the same way, sugar," said Chester. "You not bein' here with us . . . well, it just wouldn't be the same, that's all."

Hazel nodded. "An' I know that Pawpaw and Monroe and all the rest would feel just the same. Plum brokenhearted."

"But this could be a way back to the river," Celeste argued. "I can get back . . . home."

"*Back* home?" Hazel replied. "I thought you *were* home."

Celeste paused. So much had happened since she'd left Oakley Plantation. Her head was crowded with a thousand new things.

She thought of Rosebud, and steamboats, and the adventure on the river. She thought of life in the hollow, with brilliant fall colors and icicles and snow-drifts.

She thought of her friendship with Abe, and of helping him, in her small way, to read and to write.

Her memories of Joseph and Lafayette and Oakley Plantation were becoming blurred and fuzzy, like they were stumbling down a tangled path.

Her attic home in the house far down the Mississippi now seemed like something past, not something to return to. She would never forget her friends Joseph and Lafayette and Violet, but they were then. Abe and Chester and Hazel and all of her new friends in the holler were *now*.

It made her feel happy and sad, at the same time.

She wondered what home was. She thought of Chester and Hazel's swaying, leafy aerie, and of Forest and Chloe's dark but cozy underwater dome. *Very different*, she thought, *but so perfect*.

She closed her eyes, remembering her own home

under the soft, velvety warmth of Rosebud's ear.

She thought of Abe's little wooden box and the flannel rag. Snug and warm and protected.

"I guess home is where you find happiness," she said to herself. "Home is where love lives."

Hazel called down from her perch on the hickory limb. "Sweetheart, I think you'd best just stay here with us. We're family!"

She smiled.

Maybe Hazel was right. Maybe she had been home all along.

Celeste covered quite a bit of territory, for a mouse. A trip today from New Orleans, Louisiana, to Louisville, Kentucky, takes less than two hours by plane. When Celeste took a similar route on the Mississippi River on a steamboat, it took nearly a month!

Such a long trip was an expected, normal thing. It wasn't easy to travel in the early 1800s. A steamboat heading upriver was fighting a relentless current, as well as an endless barrage of snags and sandbars. And those snags and sandbars were constantly changing; every big storm that washed down the Mississippi River created a new set of challenges. It took a very skilled pilot to maneuver the heavy, cumbersome boats through the Mississippi. It was a real-life obstacle course.

Before the invention of the steam-powered engine, people relied on wind or paddles to travel across the water. Steam power was new and exciting . . . the latest thing in high-speed travel. A boat had to carry an enormous amount of firewood to stoke the engines. And those engines were in no way perfect. They were constantly breaking down and being repaired . . . or exploding!

There weren't many roads back then, but the Mississippi River was like a giant highway. River travel was the fastest way to get around at that time. Large communities like New Orleans or Natchez were bustling, busy places, but most of the towns along the Mississippi were little more than muddy collections of shacks, with wharves or docks to attract boats. Although European settlers were making more and more of a mark on the Mississippi Valley and the Midwest, it still would have been possible for Celeste to have seen Native Americans in the area.

As Celeste made her way up the river into Indiana, she would have sensed major changes in the landscape. There was no more flat, sandy terrain like that around Oakley Plantation, but rather rocky hillsides and gently sloping valleys. American chestnuts and yellow poplars would have replaced the live oaks and Spanish moss of Louisiana.

At that time, there were many animals in North America that were struggling with an increasing human population. One of them was the American beaver, highly sought after for its pelt. Beaver skins were made into beaver hats, which were very popular as a fashion statement in the early 1800s. The beaver was facing extermination. Fortunately, beaver-skin hats became less trendy and were replaced with ones made of silk.

There were tree species heading toward extinction, too. Celeste experienced her first deciduous autumn with an abundant crop of acorns and other nuts, called "mast." Especially abundant was the American chestnut. The chestnut tree was among the most dominant species of tree in the eastern half of North America. Chestnut meat was nutritious,

and because the chestnut was so plentiful, it was an extremely important food source for many, many animal species. But it was the victim of a fungal blight that started in the early 1900s, and billions of chestnut trees died. The loss of the chestnut greatly affected wildlife populations. It had been one of the most majestic and important trees of the eastern forests.

As was the eastern white pine. White pines grew straight and tall, and the wood was valuable, so they were marked and cut for lumber. Many a ship's mast was made of white pine. It was so overharvested that only a very small percentage of its original population still exists, and very few of them are of the height and girth of the great white pines that Hazel and Chester scrambled up and down.

Celeste found herself in southern Indiana, and there she just might have met Abraham Lincoln (1809–1865). He was a boy when this story takes place, living on a meager ten-acre homestead in Indiana. His birth mother had died of "milk sickness" (an illness caused by drinking the tainted milk of a cow that has eaten a certain plant, snakeroot). His father, Tom Lincoln, had remarried, to a widow named Nancy Hanks.

Nancy, who had three children of her own, was very kind to Abe, and very encouraging, and has been given much of the credit for getting Abe to read and write.

His formal education was scant, with only a few months' worth of schooling from trained teachers. Basically, he was self-taught, with help from his stepmother. The Lincolns were poor, and lived in an isolated area with few of the "niceties" of modern life. Most of the books he read and studied were borrowed from more prosperous neighbors, and he had to walk long distances to borrow them. But Abe developed an immense joy of reading; sometimes he would become very immersed in a story and forget his chores altogether. He was so studious that family and friends feared he would become a little "tetched" in the head!

Although the character of Celeste is a made-up one, it would not have been unlikely for Abe to meet a mouse like her while he was chopping wood. Abe undoubtedly ran across many, many mice during his life. He was very acquainted with the birds and mammals that lived in the eastern deciduous forest. He loved and respected them. There are stories of Abe rescuing baby birds that had fallen from their nests, or of his refusing to shoot at wild turkeys. His love of animals continued all of his life.

Of course, there are no records or letters or even oral histories of Abe ever having had a mouse for a pet. But I like to imagine Celeste scurrying across the book he's reading, or nestled in his vest pocket as he's thinking in front of the fire, with the wind howling outside.